INCREDIBLE PRAISE FOR
MARCIA MULLER

Recipient of
the Private Eye Writers of America Lifetime Achievement Award
and the Mystery Writers of America Grand Master Award

"Her stories crackle like few others on the mystery landscape." —*San Francisco Examiner & Chronicle*

"One of the world's premier mystery writers."
—*Cleveland Plain Dealer*

"Muller undoubtedly remains one of today's best mystery writers." —Associated Press

"[Muller is] adept in writing about the hard-boiled detective...Sharon McCone is compelling and endlessly interesting." —*Asbury Park Sunday Press* (NJ)

"A prime Muller mystery." —*Booklist* on *The Breakers*

"Outstanding...[an] exciting climax."
—*Publisher's Weekly* (starred review) on
The Color of Fear

"If you are ever in trouble, you want [Sharon McCone] to have your back. She...truly has a heart of platinum. Fans will enjoy cruising the city's streets with her once again." —*Booklist* on *The Color of Fear*

THE
BREAKERS

Sharon McCone Mysteries
By Marcia Muller

THE COLOR OF FEAR
SOMEONE ALWAYS KNOWS
THE NIGHT SEARCHERS
LOOKING FOR YESTERDAY
CITY OF WHISPERS
COMING BACK
LOCKED IN
BURN OUT
THE EVER-RUNNING MAN
VANISHING POINT
THE DANGEROUS HOUR
DEAD MIDNIGHT
LISTEN TO THE SILENCE
A WALK THROUGH THE FIRE
WHILE OTHER PEOPLE SLEEP
BOTH ENDS OF THE NIGHT
THE BROKEN PROMISE LAND
A WILD AND LONELY PLACE
TILL THE BUTCHERS CUT HIM DOWN
WOLF IN THE SHADOWS
PENNIES ON A DEAD WOMAN'S EYES
WHERE ECHOES LIVE
TROPHIES AND DEAD THINGS
THE SHAPE OF DREAD
THERE'S SOMETHING IN A SUNDAY
EYE OF THE STORM
THERE'S NOTHING TO BE AFRAID OF
DOUBLE (with Bill Pronzini)
LEAVE A MESSAGE FOR WILLIE
GAMES TO KEEP THE DARK AWAY
THE CHESHIRE CAT'S EYE
ASK THE CARDS A QUESTION
EDWIN OF THE IRON SHOES

Standalones

CAPE PERDIDO
CYANIDE WELLS
POINT DECEPTION

THE
BREAKERS

Marcia Muller

GRAND CENTRAL
PUBLISHING

NEW YORK BOSTON

Copyright © 2018 by Pronzini-Muller Family Trust
Excerpt of *The Color of Fear* copyright © 2017 by Pronzini-Muller Family Trust

Cover design by Blanca Aulet
Cover photograph by f11/Shutterstock
Cover copyright © 2018 by Hachette Book Group, Inc.

Grand Central Publishing
Hachette Book Group
1290 Avenue of the Americas, New York, NY 10104
grandcentralpublishing.com
twitter.com/grandcentralpub

Originally published in hardcover and ebook by Grand Central Publishing in August 2018

First Mass Market Edition: March 2019

Grand Central Publishing is a division of Hachette Book Group, Inc. The Grand Central Publishing name and logo is a trademark of Hachette Book Group, Inc.

The publisher is not responsible for websites (or their content) that are not owned by the publisher.

The Hachette Speakers Bureau provides a wide range of authors for speaking events. To find out more, go to www.hachettespeakersbureau.com or call (866) 376-6591.

Library of Congress Control Number: 2018943207

ISBN: 978-1-4555-3893-5 (hardcover), 978-1-4555-3895-9 (ebook),
978-1-4555-3894-2 (mass market)

Printed in the United States of America

OPM

10 9 8 7 6 5 4 3 2 1

To Bill, always

THE
BREAKERS

SATURDAY, AUGUST 6

1:27 p.m.

The southwestern part of San Francisco, where the Pacific washes upon Ocean Beach, is known by long-term residents as the Outerlands, or Out There by the Beach. Where surf meets sand, impenetrable fog frequently flows in, making the horns under the Golden Gate Bridge moan dolefully. The average temperature is in the midfifties—chilly at best—and fast-moving riptides are a hazard that have caused a number of experienced swimmers and surfers to be swept away and drowned. Still, the swimmers and surfers persist, refusing to allow the sea to prevail.

Above the beach, the Great Highway slices north and south, separating the dunes from the houses on Forty-Eighth Avenue in the Outer Sunset district. By and large, the homes there are small but well-kept, except for the occasional monstrosity—a fully rigged pirate ship or a model of the *Santa María* that rears its ugly head as if its builders had been trying to make a statement.

About what? I've often wondered. I've never been able to figure that one out.

I arrived at the building called the Breakers, on El

Jardin de la Playa—the Garden of the Beach, although most locals simply call it Jardin Street—twenty minutes early for my appointment with a man called Zack Kaplan, who wanted to show me something "truly bizarre."

"Run-down" would be a better term to describe the place than "bizarre." The Breakers was undistinguished to say the least: gray aluminum siding blistered by the sea winds; a roof that was shedding its shingles; sliding aluminum-sash windows that were too tiny and high up to take advantage of the sea view. The ground around it was gravel, mostly washed away to mud; there were no trees or shrubs or anything that pretended to be landscaping.

Instead of waiting in my car, I decided to stretch my legs. The weather was overcast, windy, so I zipped my jacket higher. Then I walked down to the Beach Chalet Brewery and Restaurant and crossed the highway to stand at the seawall, salt spray and sand peppering my face, looking out at the waves and a few hardy souls walking along the beach.

I'd set the appointment with Zack Kaplan at the request of my former neighbors and friends Trish and Jim Curley. They were vacationing in Costa Rica and neither they nor their son, Sean, had been able to contact their daughter, Michelle (Chelle to her friends) on her cell, her computer, or the phone at the Breakers, the building she was currently rehabbing. Zack Kaplan was one of the two remaining tenants, and he hadn't been able to reach her either.

Chelle, at twenty-three, was an up-and-coming restorer of old buildings and very conscientious; no way she would leave her cell off or fail to respond to a call from her parents. Would I check on her? Trish had asked.

Chelle was one of my favorite people. When I'd first moved next door to her family, she'd volunteered to bring in packages and feed my cats during my frequent absences; later, in a period when I couldn't drive, she'd been my chauffeur; she'd even helped on a couple of my cases, until her parents had found out and forbidden her the joys of private investigation. She was smart, innovative, and always there for those who needed her. I wanted this to be one time I was there for her.

At five minutes to two I walked back to the Breakers. Three minutes more passed, and then a battered olive-drab Jeep pulled up. A man in jeans and a thick wool shirt got out and came toward me.

"Ms. McCone?" he said. "I'm Zack Kaplan."

Kaplan had a narrow, bearded face and friendly brown eyes. Black hair stuck out from under his knitted ski cap. He wasn't tall—only a couple of inches over my own five-foot-six—but I sensed a strength in his wiry body.

We shook hands. "I see you found the building all right," he said. "Pretty grim, huh? But when I moved in, it was all I could afford. Now I'm in the grips of lethargy."

That building would make me lethargic too.

I asked, "Still no word from Chelle?"

"No, nothing. I'm starting to get alarmed."

"Me too. I understand Chelle is both rehabbing and living here."

"Yeah. Personally, I think she's nuts."

In a way I did too. But Chelle really got into her

work, and described living in a derelict building as a way of "getting at its soul."

"She have anybody there with her?" Chelle sometimes asked her current boyfriend to stay with her and pitch in.

"A guy named Damon for a week or so, but he split."

"Are you and she...?"

"No, we're just friends. My life's complicated enough without romance entering the picture."

"So you've known her how long?"

"Just since she moved in in May."

"Has she made much progress on the rehab?"

Zack looked troubled. "Not much. First there was Damon, who broke more stuff than he fixed. Next Al Majewski and Ollie Morse. They're good workers, had been on the crew of one of her other jobs in the past. But if she doesn't show up and give them their back pay, they'll have to look for other employment."

"Stop a minute—who's Damon?"

"I never did get his last name. He and Chelle had a thing going, but not for very long. Damon started telling her lies about Al and Ollie stealing from her. But she found out otherwise and gave him the ax."

"Do you know where I can find him?"

"No idea." Zack sighed. "I don't know what's going to happen to the place. The owner gave Chelle a long escrow, until she could get her final payment from her last rehab job, but it's due to close next Friday. The electric and water bills are overdue. I paid some of them—after all, I'm the only one using the utilities— but I'm a student at SF State, and I can't keep it up indefinitely."

"You said on the phone it's been a week since you've seen Chelle?"

"A week ago tomorrow. Last Sunday."

"She gave you no indication that she was planning on taking a trip? Visiting a friend or family?"

"No."

"What did she take with her? For instance, clothes for a warm or a cool climate?"

"Nothing."

This was bad—Chelle loved clothes, and her wardrobe, while sometimes eccentric, was stunning.

Zack added, "Her laptop and cell are gone, her backpack, money, and ID too."

"Well," I said, more heartily than I felt, "let's see what we can find out."

As we walked over to the building, Zack asked, "You're a licensed PI, right?"

"Yes." I handed him one of my cards.

"That kind of exciting work fascinates me."

"It's not as exciting as books and film make it seem."

"But still, unraveling the circumstances of crimes, getting at the truth, seeing that the bad guys get theirs…"

"Sitting on your butt during long stakeouts, dealing with difficult clients, and writing reports too."

"Every job's got its drawbacks."

"Let's go inside and check Chelle's apartment."

"Uh, it's not really an apartment."

"What is it, then?"

"You'll see."

The interior of the building was musty—the smell a combination of stale sea air, mildew, and dust. We entered by what Zack called the lobby, although there was no reception desk, furnishings, or tenant mailboxes. The walls were faded beige, and the worn carpeting had once been vivid with the bright pink, red, and yellow of overblown daisies. The flowers were faded now, their petals begrimed.

Zack whispered, "Like I said, pretty grim."

"Why are you whispering?"

He shrugged. "When I come in by this part of the building it has that effect on me. Like I don't want to wake anybody—or any*thing*—up."

A stairway—partially collapsed—rose to the second floor, a long first-floor hallway to the left of it. Zack led me to a door halfway along the hall and pushed it open. Inside was what looked to be an ordinary living room containing only a few mismatched and worn pieces of furniture. I frowned.

Zack noticed my look and said, "In the bedroom."

The bedroom was empty except for a sturdy stepladder that stood in its middle. Above it was an open trapdoor. "I'll go first," Zack said, "and give you a pull up."

In a few quick steps he disappeared through the trapdoor. A blazing light came on up there. I started up the ladder and he helped me climb through the hole.

An entire low-ceilinged room existed there between the two floors. I blinked against the harsh light and looked around.

"This building was a nightclub, cathouse, and bar all through Prohibition and up to 1944," Zack said. "The elite of the city flocked here, but then it went out of style. The building was sold and resold, but none of the owners could revive the nightclub trade, and thirty years ago one of them chopped it up into apartments. He didn't bother to renovate this floor because providing access would be too expensive. There used to be stairs, but vandals tore them out. This is where Chelle's been sleeping." He led me to a nook between two heavy support beams where a sleeping bag and fluffy pillows rested on an air mattress.

Chelle might have been camping out here, but she was doing it in style: a coffee machine was plugged into a nearby outlet; a small TV sat on a table at the foot of the bed; her clothes, in bright colors and exotic materials, hung on a pole. I fingered a cape trimmed with beaded braid that I particularly liked.

"Well," I said after a moment, "this place doesn't look so bad."

"Not this part, no." There was a dark note in Zack's voice. "But look over here." He went about six feet away and moved aside a Japanese screen that I recognized as having been in Chelle's bedroom at her parents' house on Church Street. What it revealed made me recoil.

The wall there was covered with old wanted posters, artists' renderings, photographs, and newspaper articles on some of the worst mass murderers in California's history. Jack the Ripper had never set foot in the state, I hoped, but you couldn't have a wall of horrors without him. The drawing wasn't a good one, but what could anybody do with a subject who had never been seen? Other killers, most of them from the past few decades, carried out the ugly theme: The Zodiac and Zebra killers of the 1970s. Charles Manson and his girls. Dan White, who in 1978 assassinated Mayor

George Moscone and Supervisor Harvey Milk. Jim Jones, who in the same year led more than nine hundred of his Peoples Temple followers to commit suicide at their compound in Guyana. The godfather of the Oakland drug trade, Felix Mitchell, who was lionized at his 1986 funeral. Gian Luigi Ferri, the 101 California Street shooter. Scott Peterson, now under death sentence for the 2002 Christmas Eve killing of his wife, Laci, and their unborn child, whose bodies he had then dumped into San Francisco Bay.

I shuddered. "How could Chelle live with this?"

He shrugged. "The reason for the screen."

"But she had to know it was there."

"Some of us are braver than others, I guess."

"She certainly didn't assemble the wall."

"God, no. It's been here for a long time—since before I moved into the building, anyway."

"Then who did?"

"Don't know. This unit had been empty for a while when Chelle took it over."

And now Chelle's gone missing.

I said, "My firm will take over payment of the utilities till her parents decide what to do. I'll need the name of the person Chelle's buying it from."

"That's easy—it's Cap'n Bobby. He runs a fish taco shop a couple of blocks away."

"Thanks, Zack. And thanks for your time and information."

"No worries. I'm with you—all I want is Chelle safely back here."

I thought, *A good man*, if *he's been completely honest with me.*

3:54 p.m.

Cap'n Bobby's fish taco shop was on the last block of Jardin Street, where it dead-ended at a steep, rocky scarp. Chunks of old concrete and boulders lay below it; at the top, juniper boughs stirred in the cold wind. On this gloomy day, Cap'n Bobby's Harbor—painted in a garish abstract pattern of orange, green, yellow, and blue with an occasional dash of pink thrown in— seemed a pleasant, if odd, oasis. I pushed through the double doors, whose handles resembled ships' wheels.

Inside was a long, dim room with a bar along the left side and tables opposite. The only light came from neon beer signs—Coors, Bud, Rainier Ale—and a few fixtures wrapped in thick nautical rope. There were only two customers, sour-looking old men hunched on stools at the opposite end of the bar. A cheerful, apple-faced man of around sixty rolled toward me in a customized wheelchair. At least I thought it was customized; I'd never seen one with such large side pockets or a huge tray mounted between the armrests in the front.

He saw me studying it and said, "I designed the way it's outfitted by myself. What I wanted was something I could store my whole damn life in—and I very nearly succeeded." Then he extended his hand. "Cap'n Bobby O'Hair. You must be Sharon McCone."

"How do you know...?"

"Zack Kaplan called me, said you'd be over. Told me you're worried about our young friend Chelle Curley."

I nodded. "You're selling the Breakers to her?"

"Yeah. I gave her the go-ahead to move in and start the renovations. She didn't have to do much to persuade me; building's an albatross, always has been."

"Why'd you buy it in the first place?"

"I was hoping to use it as a low-cost refuge for disabled vets like me." He motioned at his legs. "But I couldn't get the government funding I'd been counting on, and when my own savings nearly ran out, I said fuck it—pardon my French—and let people like Kaplan and Pincus and a bunch of derelicts move in. Kaplan's a real right guy, but the others—vandals, thieves, God knows what else."

"And Pincus?"

"Magician. God knows how he earns a living at it, but at least he pays his rent on time."

"What can you tell me about Chelle's stay there?"

"She's been in and out of here since May, when she started living in that old wreck. My lord, but that child can eat! She's partial to my fish-and-chips, but pretty much anything will do."

"When did you last see her?"

He considered. "This past weekend. Saturday, maybe."

"Did she say anything then about planning to go away for a while?"

"Not a word. Escrow's due to close on Friday, and she knows she needs to be on hand with the final payment."

"Was anyone with her that day?"

"No. She was alone, like usual."

"She had a man named Damon helping her for a while. Do you know him?"

"No. I heard about him, but she never brought him

here or mentioned him." Cap'n Bobby paused. "Look, you going to stay a while, sit down, take a load off."

I sat at the table next to his chair.

"You want something to eat? A beer, glass of wine?"

A drink sounded good right now. "I'll take a glass of white wine, thank you."

He motioned in shorthand to an Asian waitress who stood at the end of the bar. She came over quickly with my drink.

"Zack said you wanted to hear more about the building," Cap'n Bobby said.

"And its former tenants."

"I've got a ledger someplace that gives the names and dates for all of them for the past ten years. I'll be glad to let you have it."

"Thank you. Now, I've met Zack—"

"He's a good guy and the last tenant left. Unless you count Tyler Pincus, who's hardly ever there. Comes and goes, stays on the first floor."

"Did Chelle know him?"

"Friendly little thing like her? Sure she did."

"Were they...?"

"Involved? No way. Tyler's as gay as a mariachi band on *Cinco de Mayo*. He's also a little nuts."

"How so?"

"Fancies himself a wizard. Manic, but harmless."

"How can I reach him? I'd like to ask him if he's heard from Chelle."

"Hmmm. There's this bar over on Noriega Street, near Forty-Sixth—Danny's Inferno—where he hangs. Kind of a locals' joint. Two of Chelle's workers, Al Majewski and Ollie Morse, are regulars too. Tell Danny I sent you."

"Okay, thanks. By the way, there's something weird on the second floor where Chelle's been staying—I guess you'd call it a collage of pictures and newspaper clippings on violent criminals."

Cap'n Bobby grimaced. "Yeah, she told me about it. I guess you could call it a rogue's gallery, but the word usually connotes someone or something playful. Nothing playful about *that* display."

"You have any idea who put it up?"

"Nope. But this part of the city's always been known for its weirdos. For instance, Mooneysville."

I was familiar with the story. In the late 1800s, when the Geary Street, Park and Ocean Railway had been extended to the beach, a squatters' colony rose up where Playland, the old amusement park that was demolished in the 1970s, used to be. A man named—appropriately, as it turned out—Con Mooney started selling food and whiskey to folks who came out on the rails. Soon there were all sorts of tents and shanties from Cliff House to Golden Gate Park that sold bad food and worse drink. There were also games of chance and other hustles. Mooneysville only lasted two years before the city shut it down, and oddly enough, the people who had built the shanties actually helped the cops demolish them. Then they went on to more legitimate enterprises in more savory locations. The beach seemed pretty savory to me these days, but back then it was a con man's—or woman's—dream.

"Did Chelle seem upset about the wall?" I asked O'Hair.

"No, I guess she found it intriguing."

"And you have no idea who created it?"

"I've never even seen it. My legs gave out before I

could manage the climb. First I heard of the wall was when Chelle was inspecting the building and told me about it."

"What I've been wondering is why she would choose to sleep near that wall on the second floor, rather than in one of the downstairs apartments."

"Don't know. Maybe because the heat of the day rises from downstairs. There's no furnace in that building, and none of the fireplaces work. Electric space heaters are expensive to run. So she told me she made herself a nice, cozy nest and seemed very happy with it."

"Makes sense. So far it's been a cold summer."

In most other cities in the country, a forecast referring to a *cold* summer could be taken as erroneous. Not so in San Francisco, where the average summer temperatures often hover in the midfifties or lower.

I asked, "Cap'n Bobby, what can you tell me about Tyler Pincus?"

"Oddball character. Sometimes he chants and dances in public. He's disruptive, and Chelle wants him out of there. She posted eviction notices on his door twice, but they were ripped down."

"She have any plans to evict Kaplan?"

"No way. He's been good to her, and, tell you the truth, I think they might be kinda sweet on each other."

"You think they had a relationship? Zack said they didn't."

"Well, he ought to know."

I asked, "Do you remember anything more about the past tenants?"

"Hmmm. My brain gets kinda foggy this time of

day, but my ledger'll tell you. Li," he called to the waitress, "will you bring me that ledger that sits next to the cash box in my office?"

She disappeared through a curtained archway at the rear and emerged with a ragged, oversize book. When she handed it to O'Hair, she studied me as if she was trying to figure out what I was doing here.

Cap'n Bobby noticed her interest. "Li," he said, "this is Sharon McCone. Sharon's a private detective looking into Chelle Curley's disappearance."

"Oh, is she missing?"

"Since the weekend."

"That's not very long. She's a grown woman."

"Her parents are worried."

"Of course. Rich parents like to keep an eye on their darlings." Li turned and went back to the bar.

I said, "Where'd she get the idea the Curleys are rich? They're not."

"Go figure. Maybe she thinks they finance her rehab jobs." Bobby handed the ledger to me.

"I'll bring it back soon," I said.

"No matter. I've got no use for it any more."

"Appreciate it. Anything else you can tell me about the Breakers?"

"Plenty. Was built in 1903 by a rich man named Ellison Yardley. This area was a playground for ladies and gentlemen of the city's social set—that was before the quake of oh-six, which most of the buildings around here survived. Old Adolph Sutro was still sitting up there in his estate on the bluff. The Cliff House—I forget which incarnation it was, damned thing kept burning down—and the Baths were going strong. The Breakers fit right into that scene."

"I've heard part of the building was a restaurant."

"A fine one too. Mussels *à la marinière*, kidneys sautéed in Madeira sauce, sole Veronique, coq au vin." Cap'n Bobby smacked his lips. "There was a ballroom on the second story—where your young friend is staying—and people danced the nights away."

"And the top floor?"

"Ladies of the evening. You couldn't have a successful establishment in those days without them."

"Then what happened?"

"People are fickle. The war changed things. Able-bodied men went overseas. Women went into the aircraft plants. And after the initial excitement and joy of Johnny coming home, a new mind-set crept in. Everything and everyone became so serious: We had the bomb, the Russians had the bomb, God knows who else had it. Commies were forming clandestine cells all over the country. Silly slogans like 'Families that pray together stay together' appeared everywhere. Television had taken hold. And we had our inane fads. Remember the hula hoop, 3-D movies, sock hops, and drive-ins?"

"Well, my older brother might."

"All those changes are why that building went into decline. The first two owners tried to operate in the same way Ellison Yardley had. Didn't work; the old clientele didn't come. Some claimed the food was too heavy and expensive, others said the place was too far from the city's center. The next owner chopped it up—except for the second floor—into so-called luxury apartments. Apparently they weren't luxurious enough. When I bought it fifteen years ago, I had plans. But then I ended up in this chair—auto accident—and got some kind of staph infection that flares up from time to time. When Chelle came to me with a lowball offer, I'd about given up on unloading the place, so I told her she could have it for next to nothing. We've been working together on the blueprints for the rehab job. But now she's gone. I sure hope you can find her and bring her back by Friday. Not that I wouldn't extend the escrow. I just want to know she's okay."

So did I.

4:25 p.m.

Danny's Inferno was located on a commercial block of Noriega Street between Forty-Fifth and Forty-Sixth Avenues: small hardware store, secondhand clothing boutique, ice cream shop, pizza place. I wondered if the proprietor of Danny's had taken inspiration for its name from a neighbor, the Devil's Teeth Baking Company.

Inside, the Inferno carried out its hellish theme: glowing red fluorescent tubing shaped like a devil; orange neon flames flaring above the bar; Beelzebub masks on the walls. Interspersed were occult symbols: the sun cross, celebrating the paganism of the Iron Age; pentacles, prominent in European witchcraft; the hex signs that carry on even today. Odd place.

I took a stool at the bar. I'd drawn stares from a few of the customers and a waitress when I'd come in, but the barkeep seemed friendly. He looked somewhat like my image of Satan: wild black hair, thin, waxed mustache, spade-shaped patch of hair on his chin. He wore a red sequined vest over a black shirt.

I said, "Is that your work uniform or do you always wear it?"

He laughed, startling a couple seated two stools away. "Do I look like the kind of guy who gets off on people thinking he's Satan?"

"In that outfit, yeah."

"I change into my human clothes before I leave work." He reached across the bar to shake my hand. "Danny Redfin."

"Sharon McCone."

"What'll you have?"

"Glass of chardonnay."

"Yours." He bustled along the bar, brought it back. "So what brings you to this lowly place?" he asked.

"I'm looking for Tyler Pincus."

He raised his eyebrows. "What on earth you want with him?"

I set one of my cards in front of him. He looked at it, then tucked it carefully in the pocket of his red vest.

"I've heard of you," he said. "Actually, we have a mutual friend—Hank Zahn. He's my lawyer."

"And one of my best and oldest friends. We go all the way back to college."

"I'll be damned. This really is a small city, isn't it?"

"Uh-huh. That's why I like it." And sometimes why I don't like it when trying to go about my business. "So what about Tyler Pincus?"

"He hangs here sometimes." Redfin scanned the few customers. "He hasn't been in today, though."

"What's he like?"

"Obnoxious. Always tries to be the center of attention, which is hard because nobody likes him."

"What does he do? For a living, I mean."

"Nothing. He pretends to be a magician, but he's actually a trust fund baby."

A trust fund baby living in a place like the Breakers. No accounting for tastes.

Danny said, "Yeah, I know what you're thinking. It's probably not a big trust fund—if it exists at all."

"You know where I can get hold of Pincus?"

"No, but I can take your cell number, call if he comes in."

"It's on my card. Another question: does Zack Kaplan ever come here?"

"Not too often. He's a hardworking student. But I know him. A good dude. So what's this about?" Redfin asked. "If it's not confidential."

"It isn't. The more people who hear about it the better. You know Chelle Curley?"

"Sure. She stops in sometimes."

I outlined the missing person case for him.

He shook his head. "I hope she's all right. A good kid, you know, got a lot of smarts. I could help you—ask around about her."

"I'd appreciate that. There's a guy named Damon she used to be with. Do you know his last name? Or where he lives?"

"Nope, no idea."

"What about two construction guys she hired to work on the Breakers? Al Majewski and Ollie Morse?"

"They come in pretty regular, probably they'll be here tonight."

"What're they like?"

"Nice guys, good, solid workers. Ollie's had his problems—bad war injury in Afghanistan, PTSD. Al's his best buddy, looks after him."

"Let me know if they do come in. Now, what about this Damon? What's he like?"

"You want the good or the bad first?"

I shrugged, and Redfin went on.

"He's a sharp-looking dude. Tall, dark curly hair, chiseled features. Personable too. Nice smile, firm handshake. That's the good side. Now for the bad: there's this thing about him, sorta like a big dog on a leash. He's behaving, friendly. He likes being patted and given treats. But you look deep in his eyes and you know that if he weren't being patted and given treats, if he weren't secure on a leash, he'd jump on you and rip your throat out. That's Damon in a nutshell."

"What else is bad about him?"

"He doesn't really like women, particularly successful, assertive women. He beat up one of my customers pretty badly last year."

I felt a stab of anxiety. "Chelle—"

"No. At least not at first. But I think he may have gotten rough with her—she had bruises on her arms the day before she fired him. But she gave better than she got: I saw him on the street with his backpack crammed with all his stuff, and he had one beautiful shiner." Redfin shook his head. "Why is it always the good ones like Chelle who get the short end of the stick? People who are trying to make a difference—and not just for themselves, but for others too? Why do bad things always happen to them?"

His questions bothered me; I had no answer for

them. And I felt as though he'd closed the book on Chelle, expected never to see her again. Happens a lot with runaways in this city, and we tend to downplay it. But when it happens to one of your own...

5:51 p.m.

The fog had moved in, so heavy that it felt almost like drizzly rain. In August, the interior of the Bay Area can heat up to triple-digit temperatures; people would be sweltering in places like Walnut Creek, Danville, and the great agricultural valleys. But here I had to put up the hood on my rain jacket.

I was at a loss for what to do next. Until I heard from Danny Redfin, I couldn't try to chase down the two men, Majewski and Morse, who'd been working for Chelle. Damon, her rejected boyfriend, might be easier to trace, but I hadn't the abilities; I relied too heavily upon the skills of my nephew, Mick Savage, and his second in command in our research department, Derek Frye, in pinning down information from Internet sources. But now Mick was unreachable, on a well-deserved vacation to the Australian Outback—by himself, being an adventurous soul—and Derek was dealing with a family crisis in southern California. It would be difficult to corral any other member of our research department on a Saturday night.

I didn't want to go home. My husband Hy was on the East Coast—Boston—conferring with a client. Our cats, Alex and Jessie, had been alone all day, so I called the pet-sitting service we used, but they didn't answer. By now the feline hunger alarms would be going off.

So I did the responsible pet owner thing and went home to feed them.

I was just putting the latest thirty-pound bag of cat kibble into the pantry when I received a pleasant surprise: a call from my birth father, Elwood Farmer, a nationally celebrated artist who lived on the Flathead Reservation in Montana. Elwood hadn't even known he had a daughter when I caught up with him in my search for my roots, but he'd taken to me—the product of a one-night stand with a visitor to the rez—and to his new paternal role with zeal.

Tonight he said, "How's that mother of yours?"

"Which one?"

It was our usual opening gambit. Ma—my adoptive mother—was a budding watercolorist and lived on the Monterey Peninsula; Saskia Blackhawk—my birth mother—was a high-powered attorney for Indian rights in Boise.

"Katie." I detected a somber note in Elwood's voice. "I've been thinking on her all day. Can't get her out of my mind."

"As far as I know she's fine. If you're concerned about her, I'll let you know after her weekly Sunday call."

"Maybe I'll give her a ring. Or maybe I won't. Don't want to bother the old girl."

"'Old girl'—them's killing words, you know. You worried about her, or what?"

"After that business last Christmas, you never know."

Elwood had been visiting Hy and me for the holidays

when he'd been badly beaten by a group of racists. During his long hospital stay, when he was largely unconscious, Ma had concocted a fantasy about them being lovers on the verge of marriage, but when he'd recovered from his comatose state, she'd backpedaled with an Academy Award–worthy performance. Elwood—fully recovered now—had worried about her ever since. Whether he feared that she was going insane or that she might be considering taking up residence with him, none of us knew.

The rest of our conversation centered on the doings of our large clan, and when I hung up, I reflected that it was fortunate that neither of us was a way station on the moccasin telegraph—that from-my-phone-to-your-ear, from-my-fingers-to-your-e-mail network that binds us all.

6:41 p.m.

A call from Danny Redfin. Al Majewski had just come into the Inferno. He was meeting Ollie Morse there in half an hour; did I want to join them?

I set off for the Outerlands again.

At night all the curbside parking spots in the vicinity were filled. I finally found a space three blocks away and walked back to Noriega. In spite of all the cars—which probably belonged to residents who didn't have access to scarce city garages—there weren't many people out and about. Tendrils of fog curled around the tops of trees, and my footfalls echoed loudly on the damp pavement. There were few streetlights to show the way. Even the lights in the houses were dim, the windows heavily covered. I found myself glancing warily into the clotted shadows.

The red neon glare of the Inferno made me quicken my pace. A knot of people stood on the sidewalk, smoking—which is no longer allowed in many areas of the city, which has the most stringent antitobacco laws in the nation. In spite of their exile to the cold and damp, the nicotine addicts seemed cheerful; some smiled and nodded to me. As I pushed through the door, I was greeted by a gust of warm air and Willie Nelson's voice on the jukebox. Danny Redfin waved to me.

A middle-aged, well-muscled man in faded jeans and a Black Watch plaid flannel shirt straddled a stool in front of him. Danny introduced me: Al Majewski. Al had spiky brown hair and large incisors that, coupled with his long, protruding nose and jaw, reminded me of a fox terrier. After we'd shaken hands another man joined us, a short-haired blond named Ollie Morse with a goatee. Al appeared to be sober, while Ollie was at least halfway in the bag.

"Hey," Al said, "that booth in back there just opened up. Let's grab it—easier to talk."

They led me to a booth as far from the jukebox as possible. A waitress appeared and took our orders: Chardonnay for me, Jack Daniel's neat with bottles of Anchor Steam as a chaser for them.

When she returned, she set Al's and my drinks down on the table. Ollie said, "Hey, girl, where's my order?"

The waitress produced it from behind her back.

"Damn broad thinks she's a comedian." His voice was curiously uninflected.

She pulled his baseball cap down over one ear and went away grinning.

"Smart women give me the red ass." Ollie turned to me. "I suppose you think you're smart too?"

"Not particularly."

He regarded me with peculiar pale-blue eyes. Their expression was as animated as a dead man's.

"You're lying. Smart women, they give me the—"

"Ol," Al said, "Danny asked us to talk with her."

He made a growling sound, but otherwise remained silent.

"Do you have any idea where Chelle is, why she disappeared so suddenly?" I asked Al.

He shook his head. "Neither of us has a clue. There one day, gone the next, and not a word since."

Ollie's mouth turned downward and he squeezed his eyes shut. "Chelle. Poor little Chelle."

Please don't get maudlin!

Apparently Al harbored the same fear. He pushed Ollie out of the booth, said to me, "Excuse us for a few minutes," and guided his friend to a door leading to the restrooms.

The waitress came back to the booth. "Hi, I'm Pamela Redfin, Danny's daughter. He told me about your conversation this afternoon."

She was twenty-one or -two, with long dark hair worn in blunt cut and brushed back off her face.

"Sorry about Ollie's freak-out," she added. "We get a lot of the walking wounded in here; Dad's a veteran and he welcomes his brothers and sisters in combat. Ollie, for one—he suffers from PTSD."

Post-traumatic stress disorder. That explained the blank gaze and lack of inflection.

"He's been like that since he came back from Afghanistan. Al will get him settled down and be right back."

It was a good ten minutes before Al reappeared. "Thanks for waiting so long," he said. "I had more trouble getting Ollie settled down than usual. Danny keeps air mattresses and blankets in a storage room in back for people who shouldn't be put out on the streets. Ol's kind of a regular customer."

He paused, obviously considering how much more he should tell me. "You see, you gotta understand Ollie. He don't look different from other people, but way down deep, he's kind of ruined."

"The war?"

"Yeah. Afghanistan. The things he saw and did there just fried all his circuits. Most days he functions okay, but others..." He shrugged.

"So you all look out for him."

"As much as we can. Chelle was especially nice to him—just talking, keeping him calm, bringing him the kind of candy he likes, that sort of thing. He told me when I was taking him out back that he hopes you find Chelle soon. Maybe you could..."

I knew what he was about to suggest—that I counsel and comfort Ollie—but I couldn't commit to it. I have a half brother, Darcy Blackhawk, currently in care at a psychiatric institution near Provo, Utah; his condition is severe, and after dealing with that, I have very little TLC left over.

"Chelle seems to have a lot of friends around here," I said.

"She's friendly, and it's a friendly neighborhood."

"Her friendship didn't work out so well with Damon... I forget his last name."

Al's lip curled. "Delahanty. Damon Delahanty. He's a real prick. Chelle split with him after she found out he was telling lies about Ollie and me stealing from her."

"Why'd he do that?"

He shrugged. "Maybe he wanted to take over the job, bring in people of his own. The true story got around to Chelle, and right away Damon was down the road."

"Is he still in the city, do you know?"

"No idea. But I better not catch him around here again."

"So you don't have an address or phone number for him."

"Hell no. If Ol and I knew where to find him, Damon'd be black and blue all over by now."

8:46 p.m.

Armed with what little information I'd gleaned, I went to our offices in the M&R—McCone & Ripinsky—Building to make use of my resources there.

The building, I'm sorry to say, is the least distinctive on New Montgomery Street between Market and Howard Streets in the city's Financial district. Four stories of dull red brick with very little ornamentation, it squats among such architectural marvels as the Palace Hotel and the art deco Pacific Bell Building (now home of Yelp). However, the building—whose bottom floor we rent out to various businesses—has its charms: namely, Angie's Deli and the New Sports Attire on street level, and a lovely roof garden that we reserve for ourselves. The other floors also belong to M&R and have been tastefully but not ostentatiously decorated by our office manager, Ted Smalley.

A while back, there had been a bit of controversy about the building's façade: We'd commissioned internationally known artist Flavio St. John to create a sculpture to crown the main entrance. Unfortunately what the artiste had produced looked like a pair of clamshells—one gilded and one concrete, both ugly. I was sure no respectable clam would have taken up residence in either. St. John had fled the country along with our check for the work, but we'd put a stop on it in time. And, strangely enough, the sculpture—which Hy had proclaimed "as ugly as my aunt Stella Sue's butt"—crashed to the ground one early morning when no one was around, fragmenting into thousands of pieces. It might have been a structural flaw or an accident, but was neither. Some people—including those close to me—just purely hate bad art.

And that is all I will ever reveal about the Affair of the Clamshells.

Although M&R is a 24-7 operation, most of the staff perform their weekend work from home, by either phone or computer. Tonight, however, I was surprised to hear voices in one of the offices halfway down the hallway from my own.

Patrick Neilan and Julia Rafael, office mates who were working together on a case involving retail theft, had apparently come in to write their joint report. Right now they'd left off discussing the case to talk over some problem they were having with their children. Both were single parents, Patrick with two preteen boys and Julia with a son of about eight. They often discussed child-rearing issues and shared both rides to school and the babysitting services of Julia's sister, who lived with her and Tonio. I kept waiting for a romance to bud, but it seemed neither of them wanted any entanglements—at least for now.

I went into their office and said, "Who wants to work?"

Deadpan, Patrick said, "We're already on overtime. Try doubling it."

"You wish." I pulled the ledger Cap'n Bobby had given me from my briefcase and set it between them. "Names," I said. "Lots of names. Find out anything you can about them."

Julia frowned. "On Saturday night?"

"The Internet never sleeps." As I left them, I called back, "I'll take your suggestion about doubling the rate under advisement, Pat."

I am such a pushover.

At my desk I logged on to the computer and ran a couple of checks on Damon Delahanty. No phone number, address, or other easily accessible information. It struck me as unusual, in this age when keeping connected is the be-all and end-all. Tomorrow I'd turn one of my more experienced research staff members loose on locating him. No, not tomorrow. As soon as possible.

I called my "symbolic cousin," Will Camphouse.

Maybe Will is a blood relative, maybe not, but it doesn't matter because we share our Shoshone heritage in the way tribal members all over the nation do:

with good fellowship and conviviality and also a sense
of trust and willingness to be there for one another
when needed.

I'd met Will, a creative director at a Tucson ad
agency, on the Flathead Reservation in Montana a few
years ago, when he was visiting to celebrate his grand-
mother's birthday and I was trying to track down my
Indian roots. He'd introduced me to dozens of people
who might or might not have been my relatives, some
of whom became lifetime friends. Last year, he'd relocated to San Francisco and taken up residence in
one of the condominium towers that seem to spring
up monthly in SoMa. He'd started his own business
as a consultant to ad agencies on major campaigns—
that had been his specialty in Arizona—but during the
lean months before the company took hold and started
earning a profit, he'd done some work for me, and
he was adept at computer searches. I asked him if he
wanted to join me for a drink at our favorite Marina
district bar, Jasmine's.

9:10 p.m.

Jasmine's is what I like to think of as the last of the fern
bars. In the 1980s the city's drinking establishments
had been overwhelmed with fronds hanging from ceil-
ings, draping over bars, tangling in patrons' hair, and
getting between one's lips and drink. Gradually they
disappeared—too much trouble watering the plants,
too many dead leaves fluttering down—only to be replaced with fake ferns. Fake plants—whether plastic

or silk—wear out quickly from excessive handling by customers who constantly finger them to see if they're real. Now most of the fern bars have gone out of business or shifted to other motifs, but Jasmine's has persisted. And her ferns *are* real.

Will, well dressed and handsome with his black hair and Shoshone features, turned quite a few heads at the bar. He came back to my table and hugged me. Now we turned a few more heads.

"They're probably wondering what a guy like you is doing with an old broad like me," I told him.

"Nope, they're wondering how I got so lucky."

We exchanged some small talk until our drinks came, and then I filled him in on Chelle's disappearance and what I'd learned so far.

He said, "I take it you want me to locate this Delahanty guy. And also find out more about what's-his-name—Tyler Pincus."

"Yes, but there's more. As I recall, Chelle took a driving trip early last spring and visited rehabbers and other friends across the country. I didn't think to ask her parents about it when we spoke earlier, but maybe you can find out who she saw and where she went."

"I'll call the Curleys and find out about it, talk with the people she visited. Also I'll see what I can find out about the other people you mentioned—Al Majewski, Ollie Morse, Danny Redfin, and Cap'n Bobby O'Hair."

"Do you have time for all that?"

"I've got all the time in the world when it comes to you and any friends of yours." He took out his iPhone and began making notes while I provided details.

While we were talking, my phone vibrated. Chelle's

mother, Trish Curley. Well, I'd have to talk to her sooner or later, and it might as well be here and now. Fortunately Jasmine's is a quiet, laid-back place, and nobody minds cell phone use if you don't talk loudly.

"Have you found out anything about Chelle?" she asked as soon as she heard my voice.

"Not yet, but I have some promising leads."

"Nothing but *leads*! I can't understand how our daughter can just disappear—"

There were noises that indicated Jim was wresting the phone from her. "Shar," he said, "you do what you have to. We trust you, and so does Chelle."

"Where are you?" I asked. "Still in Costa Rica?"

"Right. We couldn't get a flight out—summer vacations, you know. Actually, I'd rather we stay here—we'd go nuts at home, and we know you're there helping."

I hope so. I do hope so.

I said, "While I've got you on the line, let me ask you about a few people."

Cap'n Bobby O'Hair? Chelle had mentioned him and his fish taco place, but that was all. Of course he knew of Zack Kaplan; Zack was the man who had told them of Chelle's disappearance. Tyler Pincus? Just that he was a tenant she was trying to evict from the building she was rehabbing. Danny Redfin? Jim didn't recognize the name. Ollie Morse? No. Al Majewski? Sounded vaguely familiar, but no... "What about the road trip she took to visit other rehabbers?"

"She seemed to have had a good time on it, but we didn't get into the details. We were saving them for a time when we could get together with both Sean and her."

"Has Sean heard from her?" Chelle's brother was currently in Cebu, the Philippines, taking guitar-making lessons.

"Not a word. He's worried too."

Before we ended the call, I urged Jim to persuade Trish to stay for the rest of their vacation. He wasn't sure he could. I asked to speak to her. She was running a bath—and probably crying.

Family members can be very comforting—and equally alarming when you fear you're about to lose one.

I turned to Will. "That was the missing woman's parents. I think they'll stay down there. But you never know; Trish, like her daughter, is a very headstrong person."

"Well, maybe we'll be able to wrap things up before they can book a flight. I'll get started right away." He hugged me again and made his way through the crowd at the bar, which had grown larger.

As I was finishing my wine my cell rang again. My night for phone calls, this one from Zack Kaplan at the Breakers. "Can you come out here right away?" he said in an excited voice.

"That depends. Why?"

"Something important to show you and to tell you. Right away, okay?" He disconnected before I could say anything else.

10:27 p.m.

My car was boxed into its parking place by a Twenty-Four-Hour Pickup Service truck, and it took a good deal of horn blowing to get the driver to move it. Then I drove quickly to Jardin Street and parked behind Zack's beat-up olive-drab Jeep.

No lights showed in the old building, which seemed odd after our call. I took my big flash out of the glove box. The fog was blowing strong and wet out here by the ocean, the offshore horns moaning in a demented chorus. Again I pulled up the hood of my jacket and hurried down the street toward the door where Zack and I had entered earlier.

The door was locked. I searched in vain for a bell, then pounded on the weathered wood. The sounds created hollow echoes, but no one responded. After a couple more tries, I took out my cell and called the numbers for Zack's mobile and landline. No reply, although I could hear the landline ringing through the door.

Oh, hell, what next? It hadn't been all that long since I'd talked with Zack. So why couldn't I get into the place?

I needed to get out of this inclement weather. Maybe there was another entrance...Yes, there must be. Zack had said something as we stood in the lobby earlier about wanting to whisper when he came into this part of the building. But where else *did* he enter, then?

I pictured what I'd seen while inside the Breakers. Maybe a back door to the first story? The second was closed up tight except for the trapdoors, as far as I knew. A way in that led up to the third floor, where the "ladies of the evening" had resided? That was a good possibility. I could imagine the patrons using multiple means of ingress and egress.

I started around the old building, shining my light on it. The houses to either side, Zack had told me, were untenanted, and the thick shrubbery to the rear obscured it from the sight of neighbors on the next block. It was tough going, though. The ground was uneven; twice I had to grab on to sapling trees before I found footholds. Behind the building I was shielded from the blowing fog and could make a more careful inspection.

The flash beam revealed a set of old-fashioned cellar doors at the base of the wall—the slanted double kind that flop outward to either side when you pull them open. Strange, since cellars aren't frequently found in the city—or in California in general—particularly in loose, sandy ground like this.

These doors weren't locked. I grabbed one of them and threw it back on a creaking hinge, the clattering noise it made muffled by the fog. I leaned forward, shining the flashlight's beam on what lay below three close-set steps. Not a cellar, but a neatly shored-up tunnel that angled upward to the first floor above. I stepped carefully through the opening.

The opening was large enough for one person. The steps and the wood that braced its sides looked and smelled new, and the nails that held the pieces together were shiny. They hadn't been there long.

Who had constructed this entry? Zack? He'd implied he didn't like to enter by the lobby. Chelle? God knew she was handy with tools and building materials, but she wouldn't have dreamed of creating a tunnel to sneak into a place *she* owned. Or asked Al and Ollie to do so. If she encountered an intruder, Chelle's style was more a beat-them-off-with-a-baseball-bat approach.

I walked down the three steps onto bare earth. The

dirt-walled space was about six feet high and five feet wide; at the upper end were more steps leading up to another trapdoor.

I went up the other steps and pushed on the trapdoor, dislodging a thin shower of dirt and dried leaves and other debris. This one was also hinged and stayed open. Before I climbed up through it I finger-combed as much of the debris as I could from my hair.

The room above looked to be an industrial-size kitchen, probably from the days when the elite met at the Breakers to fill up on—what had Cap'n Bobby O'Hair said? Oh, yes: coq au vin, mussels *à la marinière*, sole Veronique. And something about kidneys. God, I loathed kidneys!

Lights. The electricity had been operating this afternoon, when I'd told Zack that the agency would take over paying the bills. I felt around the wall next to me and found an old push-button switch, and an overhead light came on faintly.

Definitely an industrial-size kitchen, one in which a talented and fast-moving chef could produce—and presumably had produced—hundreds of excellent meals. No evidence of recent use, however; both the refrigerator and the stove were disconnected.

I crossed and peered into the next room. Unfurnished, it probably had once been the dining room. The other public rooms had been cleared out too—presumably on Chelle's orders. The only sign that anything was about to happen here was a collection of tools and building supplies in the front hallway.

I stood next to the old-fashioned staircase that was collapsed in the middle and called out Zack's name, but I received no answer. Then I stood still and listened. No sounds other than the wind whistling through cracks in the walls and the normal creaks and groans of an old structure.

Zack had mentioned that his apartment was number five, halfway down the first-floor hallway. I went there and tried the door, but it also was locked. Again I called out, and received no answer.

I searched the rest of the building. Zack wasn't in any of the other rooms on this floor, or in the apartments on what I'd come to call the "ladies of the evening" floor. And a more careful look around Chelle's nook and the vast vacant space beyond showed no signs of recent habitation.

I slumped down on Chelle's mattress and thought about her.

I'd known her since she was the teenager next door, who took in my mail and packages and fed my cats when I was out of town. She'd always been industrious and precocious, working at small businesses she created—"Cat Dragging: Fat Felines Need Fitness"— and socking away her earnings to fund others. In the meantime she'd maintained an A average in school, and she'd later been accepted as a scholarship student at four top-flight colleges, including Cal Berkeley, which she attended for a year before declaring that the real world could teach her more than academia. A Cal grad myself, I had to agree with her; my own sociology degree had prepared me only for work as a security guard.

So far Chelle was doing well with her rehabbing business, but it was grueling because, as a perfectionist, she ended up doing most of the work herself. And her habit of living in the derelict buildings struck me as risky. Of course, at her parents' house she'd have run the same risk as a woman alone, because Trish and Jim traveled extensively. A minimal risk, however: I'd lived alone in the house next door to the Curleys, and the biggest risk I'd encountered was the neighborhood raccoons, which were fond of upsetting my garbage cans.

But now Chelle could be in serious trouble. Her lack of communication, especially with her parents, was totally atypical. My thoughts kept turning to some sort of horrible situation or even death...

No, don't think that way. No defeatist attitudes for you, McCone.

The words that echoed in my ears were Hy's. We'd always communicated through time and distance, so why not now?

"Right," I said aloud to him.

I considered my options. Go home and wait for Zack or even Chelle to contact me? Didn't feel right; I had my phone, they could always get a hold of me on it. Call upon members of my staff and mount a full-scale search? My people were overloaded with work as it was; they wouldn't appreciate being called out at this hour for the boss's personal problem. Badger SFPD's Missing Persons detail about both of them? No, they'd tell me to call back in seventy-two hours. No matter that she'd been gone a week and I had no proof of the exact time and circumstances of her disappearance.

Okay—stay here at the Breakers and wait for Zack to return? It seemed best; the front door was locked, and odds were that few people knew about the tunnel entrance.

The decision didn't take long; I was tired, so I'd stay here. The building was cold. I took a look at the

blankets on Chelle's bed, was glad to find that the
top one was the electric type. Chelle liked her creature
comforts.

11:01 p.m.

Sleep, as it all too often does, eluded me.

The old building creaked and groaned, cold wind
and fog seeping through its many cracks. I could hear
the roar of the waves on the beach—high tide now—
and the bellow of the foghorns had never sounded so
lonesome. I shifted restlessly on Chelle's air mattress,
smelling her favorite exotic scent—sandalwood. The
bed had been made up with fresh sheets, as if she'd
been expecting me.

After a while an edgy feeling crept over me, as if
something unnatural lurked in the huge space surrounding Chelle's cozy nook. That damned killers'
gallery hidden behind her screen?

I am not a person who dwells on her anxieties—
although God knows I've had cause for more of them
than the average person. I seldom utter the words
"spooky," "eerie," or "creepy." I believe in a sort of
ESP because Hy and I share it. From the first we've
had a connection that allows us to tune in to one another's thoughts and emotions—especially in times of
trouble. But communications with the spirits of the
dead are simply beyond me. (Although sometimes I
wonder if I'm unwilling to accept the concept of such
communication because there are certainly a number
of the dead who would like to take a whack at me.)

I breathed deeply and focused on nothing at all, as a Zen friend had recommended for relaxation. I curled up in the fragrant sheets, clutching the pillow. *Strangling* the pillow, I soon realized. This situation couldn't go on!

I got up, pulled Chelle's heavy wool robe around me, and went to confront the individuals in the killers' gallery.

11:31 p.m.

Nothing on the wall had changed. There had been no removals or additions; it looked the same as before.

But why shouldn't it? I wasn't sure why I'd expected alterations, except for a suspicion in the back of my mind that the killers' gallery might have something to do with Zack's discovery. But apparently not.

The criminals depicted there were an odd lot: different, but somehow the same, like pictures of middle-class kids in a high school yearbook. Homely, attractive. Scruffy, well groomed. Long haired, short haired. Bearded, clean shaven. Young, older. Serious, smiling. Most were familiar, but there were a few strangers.

"Ordinary" was the word that came to mind.

I could discount Jack the Ripper, since no one had actually seen him, but the photos of the Zebra killers showed young black men who could have been college students, pro athletes, accountants, or TV repairmen. The Zodiac's Identi-Kit reconstruction showed a serious-looking man with black-rimmed glasses; apparently he'd thought he possessed a literary bent, because he'd sent many taunting letters and cryptograms to the SF *Chronicle*. Charlie Manson was weird—anybody could see that, except possibly his followers. Most of them were troubled young people alienated from their families, and they came mainly from middle-class backgrounds. Scott Peterson—most ordinary-looking of all of them—had been a fertilizer salesman in the Central Valley city of Modesto; his outstanding attribute had been his excessive womanizing. The ones I couldn't place also looked on the normal side of the scale.

I scanned the first few paragraphs of the cases I was unfamiliar with: Alan Johnson, who had murdered three female students in Fresno a decade ago; Tara Smith, a nurse who had killed four of her patients at a Eureka hospital over the course of two years in the late nineties; an unknown person on the Central Coast known as the Carver because he left a bloody symbol on each of his victims. There was a reproduction of the symbol, a crude circle pierced by an arrow.

How, I wondered, could such ordinary-looking people commit such hideous crimes? Shouldn't there be some weirdness that captured one's attention? Of course, the criminals that I'd apprehended had seemed weird to me, but that was because I'd known what they were up to while I was pursuing them.

But then I spotted it, the one thing that stood out. Even the artists who had drawn Jack the Ripper and the Identi-Kit likeness of the Zodiac Killer had captured it.

It was in the eyes.

Expressionless. Flat. Vacant. Lacking emotion. In essence, nobody home.

I could imagine these people out of control: in a rage, screaming, slashing, stabbing. But I could not imagine a single one of them reaching out to touch another human being with sympathy, compassion, or tenderness. That was the divide that separated them from the rest of us.

But what had created that divide?

Something in the parent-child relationship? From what I knew, a few of the individuals had been abused, abandoned, or banished from home at formative ages. And society: Had it labeled and condemned these young people for circumstances over which they'd had no control? My sociology profs from college would've said yes. As for me, I'd had a lot more experience with types like them than the average professor, and I really didn't know. But I didn't fully buy into the parental-abuse-caused-them-to-become-psychos school of thought either.

Sometimes people are just born evil.

A sound downstairs near the front entrance froze me. Footsteps, and then someone rattled the front doorknob. No one except Zack and Pincus—so far as I knew—had a key. More rattles and a mumbled curse; footsteps going away. Probably a transient searching for a place to spend the night.

I let myself down through the open trapdoor and listened. Total silence.

Then I checked to make sure the door was still securely locked. Finally I went to Zack's apartment: still locked.

The apartments in this building were fitted with the cheapest type of snap locks, and I kept a ring of keys in my bag for just such occasions as these. I took it out

and tried them one after the other until I found one
that worked.

The apartment was empty. No sign of Zack. This
was a bare-bones place like several I'd lived in during
my college years at Cal. Worn, stained beige carpeting.
Makeshift brick-and-board bookcases. Thrift-shop
chairs. And a big-screen TV, maybe forty inches. One
can live in squalid reality, but TV and all its promises
do give relief and hope.

As I turned away, I spotted a blue envelope and
sheet of notepaper on a catchall table next to the TV.
"To All" was written on the envelope in Chelle's messy
back-slanted cursive. And on the notepaper, one single
line in her equally messy block printing:

I'VE GOT A RIGHT TO DISAPPEAR.

SUNDAY, AUGUST 7

12:02 a.m.

I've got a right to disappear.
    Why?

I took the note over to Zack's desk and turned on a high-beam light. The envelope looked shabby, as if previously opened and rumpled. By Zack before he'd run out? Was this what had prompted his excited call?

The message was puzzling in the extreme. If Chelle was so disturbed about something that she felt the need to run away, why hadn't she come to one of us— the people who loved her?

It couldn't have been a romantic problem. She'd banished Damon. Not a money problem either. Cap'n Bobby would've extended the escrow indefinitely. She had friends, family, a professional support group that she herself had founded.

Health issues? Nothing could be so bad that she couldn't have depended on us. Pregnancy? She was determined not to have kids until she was able to support them, and she'd told me she used excellent protection.

Had she done something so terrible she couldn't turn to us? The part of me that's an investigator said it was possible, but the part of me that was a friend said no way.

So that left fear.

Fear for herself? Or for someone she cared about?

Whichever, the cause had to be fear.

I double-checked to make absolutely sure the handwriting was Chelle's. Looked like, but I'm no expert on the subject. And there was something about the wording. Her personality was exuberant, spilled over into everything she did. But this note, that one single line, felt so...dead.

The word "dead" hung in my mind, and I actually waved my hand to dispel the thought.

Finally I put the note into my briefcase. I was too tired to think any more about who had delivered it or what it meant. Or to think about Zack's continued absence.

Right now I badly needed sleep.

2:17 a.m.

Sleep. Yeah, right. Wasn't in the picture for me tonight.

I lay there for a while listening to the creaks and groans and the slowly diminishing roar of the waves. Then, as I often do when I'm alone and can't sleep, I thought about Hy.

Where was he now? I didn't have any intimations of danger; my husband's schedule is as erratic as mine. On impulse I called his cell, and was glad I had. He answered right away, sounding as awake as I felt. It was a relief to hear his voice.

"McCone," he said, "what's happening?"

"Where are you?"

"Amsterdam, in a very luxurious hotel suite on a canal."

"I thought you were in Boston."

"I was, but the guy there liked our proposal and wanted me to meet with the head honcho. But I don't think you're interested in that right now. What's wrong?"

I filled him in on what I was contending with. "Any ideas?" I asked when I finished.

"If I didn't know Chelle, I'd say it was a plea for attention. But she's not like that. If she's gone into hiding, she may have left that note because she wants everybody to know she's okay."

"Hiding from who or what, though?"

"What's she been doing lately—before she started the Breakers rehab project?"

"Well, she took a few months off after the previous job. Traveled around the country visiting fellow rehabbers and friends."

"Who and where?"

"I don't have any names yet, but she drove that miserable truck of hers all the way to Vermont before it broke down; when she got back here, she borrowed one so she could haul equipment and supplies to the Breakers. In May she moved in there, and it wasn't long before the trouble with the rehabbing started."

"Trouble with Damon?"

"At first, but she threw him out when she found out he was spreading lies about her other workers stealing from her."

"How sure are you that they were lies?"

"Not a hundred percent certain yet. I've got Will working on locating Damon's present whereabouts, and he's also going to check with the people she visited on her trip, in case she mentioned anything about trouble."

"This Zack—what d'you know about him?"

"Just that he's a friend of Chelle's and the one who let me know when she went missing." I stifled a yawn.

"What about his background? What does he do for a living?"

"A professional student, I think. Will is checking into that too."

"How long has Zack been gone now?"

"Not very. I got over here pretty quick after he called me."

"No clue as to where he went or why?"

"None." This time I yawned out loud.

Hy laughed. "Sounds like you're ready for sleep now. Love you. We'll talk tomorrow."

We disconnected and I drifted off, cradled in the scent of Chelle's sandalwood perfume.

10:29 a.m.

Banging noises. Couldn't a person get any sleep—?

Groggily I propped myself up on my elbows. The space around me was shadowy. Where...? Oh, right. Chelle's bedroom in the Breakers. But who was making that unholy racket?

I got up, put on her robe, and let myself down through the trapdoor. A belt sander started up below. I peered over the banister of the defunct staircase. Ollie Morse, about to attack the hardwood floor.

"Ollie!" I called.

He looked around and then up, frowning, then shut the tool off.

"Hey," he said, "what're you doing here?"

"I could ask you the same."

"Oh, right. Nobody told you. Last night me and Al got to talking about Chelle and decided to help her out while she's gone. So we went to see Cap'n Bobby, and he told us that the floors should be first."

That didn't sound right to me. I'd renovated my former house on Church Street and done the plumbing first and the floors last. That way they wouldn't be marred by equipment being dragged over them.

"Is Al around?" I asked.

"Someplace." Ollie sounded annoyed.

"I'll find him."

But I didn't. Al was nowhere on the premises. What was it with this building? I wondered. Did it swallow people whole?

I went back to Chelle's lair and tried to do something with my hair.

No way; it wasn't about to let me. Finally I shrugged, gathered my jacket and purse, then went out for food and more information.

11:43 a.m.

Cap'n Bobby didn't look too well this morning: the whites of his eyes were red streaked and the pouches beneath them were more pronounced. He waved for me to help myself from the coffee maker at the end of the bar. When I'd collected it and sat at the table nearest him, he asked, "Anything new?"

I told him about the "right to disappear" note.

He frowned and shook his head in a puzzled way. "Funny kind of message to write, just that one line."

"I think so too."

"Where'd Zack Kaplan get it?"

"I don't know. Do you have any idea why Chelle would want to suddenly disappear?"

"No. Doesn't make any sense that she would."

I sipped coffee and set it down; it was one of those ultrasweet brews that were clogging the market lately. "Here's another odd thing: Zack seems to have disappeared too. Last night he called me and asked me to come to the Breakers right away, said he had something to show me—the note, probably—and to tell me. When I got there, no Zack."

"That's odd."

"It sure is. His Jeep's still parked outside. What can you tell me about him?"

"Well, he's lived in number five over there since he started college at SF State. Has always had money problems, but makes up on what he owes. Is helpful, fixes stuff when it gets broken." Cap'n Bobby frowned. "Zack's an all-round good guy, but I don't really know him."

"Did Chelle ever tell you what she intended to do with the building?"

"Oh, yeah. We were working together on the plans. She's going to get it in shape and then sell it to Elder-Care, one of those services that provide for the old and infirm. In this case they'll use it for disabled vets, like I was going to."

I'd heard of ElderCare; it was highly rated.

"I've seen a draft of the contract for the eventual sale," Cap'n Bobby added. "It's loaded with stipulations about quality of care; Chelle will sit on their board of directors."

So like Chelle to make sure everything was aboveboard.

I said, "There are couple of other things I'd like to talk to you about. Ollie Morse is over at the Breakers refinishing the floors. He said you told him to do them first."

His face reddened and he pounded his fist on the arm of his chair. "That idiot!" he exclaimed. "I told him no such thing. Anybody knows you do the floors last. Was Al there?"

"Ollie said he was, but I couldn't find him."

Cap'n Bobby pulled out a cell phone, punched in a number. The call must have gone to voice mail because he said, "Al, wherever you are, get back to me ASAP. You've got to rein in Ollie before he costs Chelle a fortune." As he clicked the phone off he said to me, "Don't know why Al and I put up with Ollie, but we do."

"What happened to Ollie in Afghanistan?"

"Same thing as happened to a lot of us on the battlefield. Me, it was a spinal injury when my Jeep overturned. That's not as bad as some—you adapt. But it's the injury to the mind and spirit that's the hardest to heal. Ollie's PTSD is worse than most. All the counseling I've done with disabled vets, I've yet to find any conventional—or even unconventional—treatment to use for what ails him."

"You know much about his history?"

Li, the waitress I'd met yesterday, appeared with the fish-and-chips I'd ordered. "I do," she said. "We were...close a couple of years ago. Ollie was born in Missouri—near Kansas City, I think. His parents weren't in the picture, so he was raised by his mother's folks. Lit out for LA as soon as he finished high school, wanting to be a movie star. Same sad old story of no callbacks and lousy jobs flipping burgers, and then he enlisted in the army and ended up in Afghanistan. What happened there, I don't know."

I asked, "How come he came to San Francisco?"

Li smiled wryly. "How come any of us do?"

"Good point."

Cap'n Bobby asked her, "And how close were you to Ollie?"

"Let's just say we had a thing at one time. It didn't last long." She turned and went back toward the kitchen.

"'A thing'?" Bobby grumbled. "Why can't you young folks say what you mean? 'A thing' does not raise lustful questions in the minds of those who are...slightly older."

"What would you like us to call it?"

"Something that will remind us we all were young and crazy once. Anything else you want to ask me?"

"The wall behind Chelle's screen. I'm trying to pin down how long it's been there."

"When was the last posting?"

"According to what datelines that I could see on the newspaper articles, around twelve years ago."

"Long time. What does that wall have to do with her being missing?"

"I don't know that it has anything to do with it. But something seems to have freaked her out. Do you know who created that crazy collage?"

"No."

"Who was living there in 2002, or a few years on either side?"

He spread his hands wide. "My ledger starts after that, and there was nothing about past tenants in the disclosure statement."

"And you didn't try to meet them or ask about the wall?"

"I didn't know about the wall. Even then, I wasn't so spry; I took the real estate agent's word for what was up there."

"Do you recall the agent's name?"

"Pat...something. Doesn't matter, I saw she died four, five years ago."

"Okay, but there's something I'd like you to do for me."

"Sure, I'll help any way I can."

"Good. Write a short note introducing me to any neighbors of the Breakers you know, saying I'm looking into Chelle's disappearance and it's okay to talk with me."

"Should I mention you're interested in that wall?"

"No. Just keep it short and to the point."

4:53 p.m.

By the end of the afternoon I'd met a fair number of residents of the Outerlands, and most were definitely on the odd side.

Sara Gottfried, two doors down from the Breakers: "I've been living here since my husband died in Vietnam. That's close to fifty years now. I could never quite get my life together afterwards, just stayed home with my cats—generations of them. What...? Oh, that old eyesore down the block. I haven't set foot in it. No, I don't know anything about the former tenants or a wall...Chelle? Zack? Damon? No, the names aren't familiar. I seldom go out now that Safeway delivers."

Wendall Manning, three doors away: "Yeah, that used to be a real rockin' place in the seventies. A party every night. Live bands—some of them made it big. Lots of booze. And the chicks...Yeah, I know I'm too old to be talking about chicks, but those were the days. The names you mentioned—never heard of 'em."

Alana Du Bois, at the southern end of the block: "Oh, that Wendall Manning! Old goat's tried to pinch my butt about a hundred times. Don't pay attention to anything he says. I've lived here six years and I haven't noticed anybody at the Breakers but derelicts. Zack Kaplan? Chelle Curley? Damon Delahanty? Sorry, never heard of them."

Digger Burnett, at the opposite end of Jardin Street: "You gotta excuse me; I'm all dirty, just got home from work. Drive a scoop loader down at that new tower they're tryin' to build near the Civic Center. Digger— get it? Yeah, I heard the Breakers sold. No, I never been there; I got a thing about haunted places."

Erin Moran, next door: "Haunted? Oh, God, that Digger! He's cracked in the head. The building's just there, waiting for its new life. That new owner, she's very young, but she seems to know what she's doing.

Have I seen her recently? Oh, I'm sure I have, but my memory isn't so good with dates."

Alicia Alvarez, next door to Erin: "Of course I know Chelle. She's promised to give me some cleaning work once she's got that building torn apart. And Zack? We had a little romance a couple of years ago. A very *little* one." She giggled. "I still see him around. Tyler Pincus? Is he the one who built that tunnel into the place? I bet he is. He's weird, maybe dangerous. I cross the street when I see him coming. A collage? Oh, you mean one of those things where people paste up stuff? No, I don't know anything about that."

6:55 p.m.

The rest of the nearby neighbors either weren't home or were unfriendly and closemouthed if they bothered to open their front doors. One who called herself Lady Mary allowed as she'd once had dinner with Zack Kaplan, but that he was "a cheapskate." That was the only information I got from any of that small bunch. Finally I returned to my car and drove home, tired of ringing doorbells.

I was just putting my car in the garage at our house on Avila Street when my phone rang. Will.

"Want to meet at Jasmine's?" he asked. "I've got a bunch of stuff to go over with you."

"Great." I thought of Jasmine's extravagant nacho platters, and my stomach growled. It had been a long time since the fish-and-chips at Cap'n Bobby's. "Where are you?"

"The office."

"Well, I'm home, so even walking I should get to Jasmine's before you do. Anything I can order ahead for you?"

"An IPA."

"What kind—they've got four or five dozen on tap."

"Surprise me."

7:15 p.m.

It was an unusually long time before Will arrived at the fern bar. So long I feared that the Sculpin IPA I'd ordered for him would grow warm.

"What kept you?" I asked when he appeared.

"I ran into Ted and Neal. They were going to a friend's wedding and dropped by to pick up some champagne Ted had sequestered in his desk. Neal was all duded up in proper formal wear, but Ted..." He shook his head, laughing. "He had on the damnedest getup."

"Not Botany 500 again!"

"Yep. The jacket had a black background overwhelmed by vertical stripes—mauve and red and deep purple. Between each stripe were little glittery stars. And, to top it off, the lining!"

"Gaudy?" I said.

"Bright lime-and-gold paisley."

"And the pants?"

"Conservatively styled in banana yellow."

"Ouch! Shoes?"

"Penny loafers with an unpleasant yellow-brown sheen."

"Oh, my!" I put my hand to my eyes, warding off the image.

Will said, "You've gotta see it to believe it."

"No, I don't." I signaled for a glass of wine.

Ted Smalley was my office manager, had been with me since I worked as chief—and only—investigator at All Souls Legal Cooperative. When the poverty law firm folded, he'd come along to manage my new operation, McCone Investigations, in drafty old Pier 24½ next door to the SF fireboat station. He was with me still.

For years, Ted had been going through various fashion statements: Edwardian, grunge, Victorian, cowboy, you name it. The most recent was a takeoff on the old *Mannix* TV show, featuring garish sports coats from the now-defunct—thank God!—clothier Botany 500. Fortunately, his present work overseeing all the internal operations of M&R didn't require much public contact.

Ted's husband, Neal Osborn, an online seller of rare books, had a vastly different sartorial style: except for on the handball court or lounging around home, he was usually clad in vested suits that he had made by a tailor in London and beautifully tooled leather footwear. It was unfortunate, we often said, that Neal had so little reason to meet his clientele in person.

Still chuckling at the vision of Ted in his finery, I took out my phone and turned its recorder on. "So what do you have for me?" I asked Will.

Plenty, as it turned out.

"Start with Zack Kaplan," Will said. "Born in Fort Worth, Texas, thirty-eight years ago. Spotty work history, mostly menial jobs. Currently a senior at SF State. Pretty old to be attending college."

"A lot of people go back when they can afford to."

"My feeling is that Kaplan is a professional student—one of the kind who feel safe in an academic environment but can't face going out into the real world. He went to four different schools before settling at State: Long Beach, Fresno, Chico, and City College. Declared several different majors: history, English, French, mathematics, and Sanskrit."

"Sanskrit! Why?"

Will shrugged. "Maybe the classes met at the right time of day. Anyway, his parents are deceased. No siblings, no close relatives. A few friends, whom I'm trying to track down."

"Enemies?"

"Not any who would admit to it."

"How is he supporting himself now?"

"Part-time bartender at various places, part-time deliveryman for a floral shop called Rosie's Posies."

"Military service?"

"None."

"Anything else on him?"

"That's it, till I hear from his friends. On to Damon Delahanty. He's somebody Chelle is well off without. Delahanty was in prison until four years ago. Armed robbery."

"Oh? Details?"

"He tried to rob a convenience store in Vallejo but the owner was quick with a gun, shot him in the leg. When the cops ran a background check, it turned out he'd been suspected, but never indicted, for a couple of similar crimes in the Bay Area."

"Did he serve his full sentence?"

"Yep."

"See if you can get any more on him from the DOC."

"Will do. These workers of Chelle's—Al Majewski and Ollie Morse—I know something about Morse: Was born in Kansas City, Kansas. Orphaned when both parents were killed in a car wreck and raised by his maternal aunt, now deceased. Dropped out of high school in his junior year and headed for Hollywood. Got caught up in the usual sleaze and scams and no callbacks on the legitimate jobs. He was off the radar for a while until he joined the army close to ten years ago."

"And Al Majewski?"

"His background is pretty sketchy too. Born and raised in Idaho, left home at fifteen, and worked construction in several western states before joining the army. Neither Morse nor Majewski has ever been married."

Will sipped some of his IPA. "Now, Cap'n Bobby O'Hair. Honest as the day is long. He's originally from New Hampshire. Moved out here to get to better weather. Used to work at a dive bar on the north waterfront called Tugbert's, inherited some money from an aunt back east and bought it. When it got to be fashionable—and by now you know that Bobby's not a fan of the fashionable—he sold out and bought his current place, as well as that derelict building on Jardin Street. He's never been married, but a lot of ladies come and go. Is generous with those who need help, kind, and generally well liked."

"My feelings exactly. What about Danny Redfin?"

"The word on the street is that he's dealing drugs out of his bar. Mostly marijuana, some low-grade coke. But you and I know how rumors like that can get started."

I frowned. "You sound more like an undercover cop than a former ad man."

"I guess I watch too much TV. Maybe tomorrow I can get more concrete info from Danny's daughter Pamela. She's cute."

"Okay," I said. "Tyler Pincus?"

"A self-proclaimed wizard."

"Like Harry Potter?"

"Hardly. Harry's a novice compared to Pincus. Old Tyler's been plying his trade at card tricks for nearly sixty years. Back in the 1960s and '70s there was a jazz club on Clay Street near the Transamerica Pyramid called Earthquake McGoon's, and in its basement was a little place—the Magic Cellar."

"I've heard of it."

"Well, local and world-class magicians put on their acts there, and Pincus was one of them. At least he was till they threw him out."

"For what?"

"That's not clear. Must've been serious, though, because the owners and the patrons were a pretty hang-loose crowd."

"And what did Pincus do then?"

"Toured around the country a bit doing his close-up card tricks, but mainly he faded into obscurity. He's kept his apartment at the Breakers since the eighties, but he's hardly ever there, so he must be getting gigs someplace. I've heard—in spite of the popularity of young Harry Potter—that magic's on the wane. Probably because the reality we're confronting these days is too frightening."

"I'd think it would be the other way round. Escapism. Stick our heads in the sand."

"Have you been assuming the ostrich position lately?"

"It's tempting. But no, I haven't."

"And none of us will, until we exorcize the demons in our world—and you know who they are."

"Oh, yes, I do."

9:47 p.m.

Will and I were having a second round of drinks when a friend of mine and another regular at Jasmine's, Jamie Strogan, stopped by our table. Strogan, a heavy-set man with straw-colored hair that stood up in unruly spikes, was an inspector with the SFPD's Homicide detail.

"So, Sharon," he said, "I hear you're infringing on our territory again."

I introduced him to Will and said, "I don't understand."

The lines around Strogan's eyes crinkled. "Just a joke. In one of the coffee-break rooms at the Hall there's a scorecard: 'Us: 21, McCone: 200.'"

"Hardly that big a ratio!"

"Yeah, exaggerated. But somebody started the card a long time ago, and now when you get a hit, one of us updates it—allowing for inflation."

I knew who had probably started the tally: my

former lover and old friend, Lieutenant Greg Marcus, now retired and living in the Gold Country. It was through him that I'd met and become friendly with Strogan.

"Anyway," Strogan added, "a colleague in Missing Persons tells me you've made an inquiry for information?"

"One of my operatives did, yes. So far I've heard nothing."

"You want I should expedite the request for you?"

"If you would, I'd appreciate it."

"No problem. Of course, if you learn anything pertinent to Homicide, you'll report it to me."

"Certainly."

He took out his phone, entered a reminder. "Back to you soonest."

"Will you join us for a drink? Will and I have been discussing mutual relatives in Montana."

"Relatives!" He waved a hand and headed toward the bar.

"That word's most always a conversation stopper," Will said.

"Isn't it, though." I fell silent, thinking of my crazy half brother Darcy and my dead brother Joey. And Ma, who seemed to be deteriorating day by day.

Will sensed my onset of depression and said, "You know, this missing person thing could be construed as fraud. Person disappears, then an accomplice comes forth, demanding money for his or her return. That note that came—purportedly from Chelle—could mark the beginning of a scam to extract money from her friends or family. The kind of girl you describe probably wouldn't knowingly be involved in it."

"But the note was in her handwriting on her stationery."

"Didn't you say there was something wrong with the writing?"

"It was...restrained."

"So she could have been under duress, or somebody faked it."

"Possibly, yes."

He went on, "Zack Kaplan's disappearance is puzzling too. Was he part of a scam and took off to wherever Chelle is being held? Or is he another victim, maybe because he knew too much? Anyhow, as you've said, our biggest priority is to locate Chelle and bring her home safely."

"Did you say 'our'?"

"Uh-huh. I'm working with you, aren't I?"

"As long as you don't have other pressing things to do."

"I don't. My new business is not exactly taking off into the stratosphere."

"Well, thanks. I'm grateful. I don't think Jamie Strogan's going to be able to galvanize Missing Persons into moving on this."

"I doubt you have enough evidence that a crime has actually been committed to rely on them."

"Probably not. But I'm glad I reported the disappearances anyway."

"Always good to leave a paper trail."

"Will, what do you think about that killers' wall gallery?"

"I really don't understand how it figures in Chelle's disappearance."

"I have a feeling it does, somehow."

"Yeah, you may be right. You want another glass of wine?"

"Why not?" I wasn't driving, and home was only two blocks away.

After he'd placed our order, Will asked, "You're not going to stay at the Breakers again tonight, are you?"

"No. Doesn't seem to be much point in it. Besides, I miss my cats and my house."

Will looked relieved. When our refills came, he touched his glass to mine and said, "To Chelle."

"To Chelle and her safe return."

11:12 p.m.

Of course, I can never leave well enough alone. Especially when it comes to a personal investigation like this one.

After leaving Jasmine's I started thinking about Zack's Jeep. Parked where it was, abutting the corner at the end of Jardin Street, it might have been ticketed and towed away, though it was probably a little too soon for that to have happened. If the Jeep was still there, I wanted to examine its contents for a possible clue to his whereabouts.

The Jeep was still there, and it hadn't been ticketed. It was a CJ-7—forerunner of today's Wrangler. I recognized the model because for most of their teenage years my older brothers had spent half their time conferring under the hood of one. Theirs, which ran only periodically, had been a muddy olive drab, perhaps once painted in a camouflage pattern, and its canvas cover was torn in various places. This one didn't have much of an edge on it: the grille was badly dented; the windshield was scored with cracks; the door gave a mild screech as I opened it; I caught my foot on a torn floor mat as I climbed in.

If Zack Kaplan had voluntarily walked away from this derelict machine, he'd been fully justified.

There were no keys in the ignition or any of the obvious places. I dug around under the seats and came up with nothing more than crumpled fast food wrappers and Styrofoam cups. A used condom surfaced from under a magazine and my ick factor rose, but I bagged it anyway for possible DNA testing.

I moved the seat forward a quarter of an inch, jiggled it to see if there was anything lodged underneath. Something shifted slightly but refused to come free. I moved the seat some more, wedging my body up against the steering wheel. Then I heard a pinging sound and whatever it was fell to the trash-covered floor. I twisted around to retrieve it, shone my flash on it.

It was a key—bent but probably still usable. I stomped on it with the heel of my boot and straightened it some. When I tried it in the ignition it turned, and the engine started right away.

So if Zack had left the Breakers voluntarily last night, why hadn't he taken the Jeep? And if his disappearance hadn't been voluntary, who had caused it and why?

And where was he now?

MONDAY, AUGUST 8

7:17 a.m.

I woke up with one cat snoring on the pillow above my head, the other nestled between my feet. When I wriggled around and reached for my phone, they both levitated and then stalked out of the bedroom, intent on the food bowl in the kitchen downstairs.

"You can wait for breakfast," I called after them. "You're both way too fat anyway."

I checked my voice mail, as I'd done on the way home from Jardin Street last night. Nothing new pertaining to Chelle or Zack. A lot of other messages had accumulated, a few of which I'd briefly listened to before. I decided to start returning them.

Hy: "Still in Amsterdam, but heading for New York tomorrow. We got the contract. Talk to you soon."

All right!

Ted: "You're going to love the new Botany 500 outfit I've scored!"

Oh, no I won't.

My younger sister Charlene, currently living in London with her second husband, Vic Christiansen, was complaining about the behavior of her youngest girls: "Molly and Lisa have driven us crazy during this visit. You want to adopt them?"

Your fault for having six kids.

My other younger sister Patsy, with kitchen noises in the background: "Ben and I have set our wedding date for November, and I've signed a lease on a second restaurant, in Sonoma this time. Didn't I tell you I'm getting closer to you guys all the time?"

And her four-star restaurant's getting closer too!

My niece Jamie, a performer like her father, country superstar Ricky Savage: "The gig in Denver went great! Want to meet me in Colorado Springs tomorrow?"

Sorry, kid—but I'll see you soon.

Nothing from Ma, who always called from Pacific Grove late on Sunday when the rates were low.

Now *that* was worrisome.

Aunt Adeline: Who the hell was she? Oh, right—a scam. She was in trouble and wanted money.

Mick, speaking in an Australian accent: "G'day. I'm here in the Outback having a cold one with some new cobbers from Halifax. Golf courses everywhere, but for me it's the wineries. Found a good cab sav yesterday and sent you a couple of bottles. Went to a great piss-up last night, and I'm still feeling kind of legless."

A quick study with dialects, the kid was, even if he'd been to a great party the night before with his new friends and was now hungover.

"Anyway," he went on, "I'll be winging your way soonest. Cheerio to all."

I tried phoning Ma, but my call wasn't answered, and I couldn't leave a message; my mother didn't believe in answering machines or voice mail. She called herself "a true Luddite." Well, I'd have to try again later.

I was about to leave for the agency when the phone rang. I picked up.

There was a pause, and then an unfamiliar female voice said, "Stay out of it, McCone. I'm warning you—stay out!"

10:00 a.m.

When I got to the agency, I glanced into the conference room. Julia and Patrick sat at the old round table. Patrick gestured to me and I went in.

Julia said, "Pat and I have been brainstorming about where Chelle Curley might be."

"Oh?" I set my briefcase down on the scarred table-top.

The round oak relic had once stood by the kitchen windows at All Souls' Bernal Heights Victorian, where it was a gathering place for many of us back in the days when we were young and idealistic and—let's face it—foolish about the cruel ways of the world. The table was covered with wine and coffee and other unidentifiable stains that would never come out. Initials and sayings were carved or deeply inked into its rough surface: *War Sucks. Racism Sucks. Stop Saying Everything Sucks! Grrrrh! Why would anybody wanna be a lawyer? Me. You* are *one.*

"Any conclusions?" I asked.

Patrick said, "Chelle has only the one brother, Sean. And her father Jim is her birth father, right?"

"Right."

"There goes the deadbeat dad theory. Also a snatch by a disgruntled former spouse of her mother."

I said, "A good idea, but the Curley family are as normal as they come."

"Says you."

"What makes you think the Curleys *aren't* normal?"

"A few things Chelle's said in my hearing: they're always traveling, and they forget to leave contact numbers; they break off conversations when she comes into a room, like they have secrets; sometimes she'd like to run away from them."

Julia said, "Tonio's taken to running away from home whenever my sister or I criticize him. Of course, we always know where he is because of the feathers."

"What?"

"He hides in an old chicken coop that belongs to the neighbors. When he comes home, the feathers are a dead giveaway."

"But what does this have to do with Chelle?"

"Maybe she had a disagreement with her parents, and—"

I shook my head. "Her parents didn't mention one; besides, she's a grown woman and probably isn't all that fond of chicken coops. But in light of this 'right to disappear' note, we'll look into possible hiding places."

"Such as?" Patrick asked.

"Well, in the area of the Breakers. Near her parents' home. Other places she's been known to frequent. How about I pull you off the deadbeat dad detail and let you handle this?"

Patrick nodded and jotted down some notes.

I excused myself and tried to call Ma again. Still no answer, so I rang Mrs. Kingsley, a neighbor who often checked up on her. No answer there, but the neighbor—no Luddite—had voice mail, so I asked her to call me back. Then I hurried to the conference room.

Ted entered the room behind me and said, "A call came in yesterday—"

"Probably from somebody wanting to revive the Botany 500 line," Julia remarked.

I silenced her with a frown.

"A call came in," Ted repeated, "but the person wouldn't identify themself. Just said they had important information about one of our investigations. They hung up when I asked who they were and never called back."

"Man or woman?"

"Woman, I think, but I'm not sure. The voice was muffled."

"Did you ask the tech department to try to trace it?"

"Yes. No luck so far."

"I'll need a copy of that call when they're done with it."

"Right."

Will had appeared on Ted's heels. "Last night Shar and I discussed Chelle's note about the right to disappear. She feels there's something odd about it."

"What seems odd?" Patrick asked me.

"The tone and handwriting. They're not her usual style. Nothing specific; you'd have to know her well to notice it."

"So it might've been written under duress."

"Exactly. You'll all be getting a copy of it and a

memo shortly, but right now I'd like to show it to you."
I flicked the button for visual display; it lowered the
screen on the far wall and dimmed the lights, and an
image of Chelle's note appeared.

They all studied it. Julia asked, "Is her writing always that bad?"

"Her signature is clear, but then I've never received
anything but cards from her."

Ted said, "Look at that."

"What?"

He got up and went to the screen. "See this? This
little squiggle here in the lower left corner."

"Squiggle" was the right word for it. It wavered,
went straight, then vanished.

I said, "It looks as if she was trying to add something else, and then the note was taken from her. Is
there any way the tech department can figure out what
she might have intended it to be?"

Ted shrugged. "It's worth a try."

I checked my watch. "Okay, I've got to go. Thank
you for coming on such short notice. Now let's get
to work." I didn't need to ask that they let me know
anything—even the smallest detail—that they found
out.

2:00 p.m.

That unfamiliar-sounding voice on the phone this
morning had kept nagging at me. I had recorded it,
but even the technology we used at M&R could not
have yielded the kind of information I wanted. Around

eleven I'd called Carolina Owens, an old friend from college who worked for a tech forensics firm. She told me to copy whatever I had. She was busy for an hour, but maybe we could meet at two for lunch at Yanni's?

I resisted telling her that I hated Yanni's. It was too hip, served too much weird, bad food, and the drinks were wildly expensive—even the Pellegrino. But she was doing me a favor, so I agreed, steeling myself for a terrible meal. Not long after two o'clock I was seated at an unsheltered table on Yanni's Bayside deck, perspiring and wondering why so many items on today's menu involved squid ink.

Carolina arrived, wearing a big picture hat that would have done Scarlett O'Hara proud. Her walk was as bouncy as it had been when we used to stroll Telegraph Avenue together, and her shoulder-length blond hair bounced in counterrhythm. We hugged, and then she seized the menu and said, "Oooh! Squid ink pasta with smoked salmon is on special. One of my favorites."

Perversely, I ordered a cheeseburger. We chatted about inconsequential topics till our meals came. Hers looked like a combination of orange bugs and long white worms swimming in black ooze. I kept my eyes on my burger, which had proved to be overcooked.

"So," she said, "you need some technical information?"

"Yes." I took the two recordings out of my bag. "This is a call I received at home this morning. The voice is unfamiliar to me. I'm wondering if there's a way you can enhance it."

"I can both enhance and possibly identify the voice for you."

Voice recognition. Of course her firm would have that capability.

She asked, "How much do you know about tech forensics?"

"Some. Refresh me, please."

"Well, I won't give you a full course in it—because we'd end up sitting here for the next two weeks—but here's the gist of what we tell clients that our experts can do."

Speaker recognition, Carolina told me, uses acoustic features that differ widely among individuals. One relates to anatomy: the size, shape, and possible malformations of the throat, nasal passages, teeth, and mouth. The second is derived from behavioral patterns, such as voice pitch, regional accents, speed and volume, and stuttering and other general speech patterns. Emotional reactions—nervousness, depression, elation, and manifestations of obsessive-compulsive disorder—can also figure in.

I asked Carolina, "Is it difficult to link all these factors to a specific individual?"

"In many cases it's impossible. But if we possess an existing template for the person, we can. I have to tell you that many of the methods of accessing templates that we don't have are not legal. You'll need to swear that you'll never reveal whatever I do for you."

Over the course of my career I'd bent and broken many a law in the pursuit of justice. "I swear."

"Okay. Templates can be recorded with the individuals' consent, either in person or over the phone. And without their consent in the same manner. Police departments do it regularly with suspects they interrogate. As do companies that are interviewing job applicants or independent contractors. If you've ever ordered a product by phone in the past few years, your voiceprint may be stored with the company and its affiliates. And your bank or stockbroker keeps it as a security feature. Firms like mine have huge libraries of templates that we buy from various sources."

"So you're telling me that anything I say on the phone or even in person can be made public."

"That's right, anything. And until this country gets off its collective ass and enacts legislation against the practice, nothing ever will be private. But that's very unlikely to happen, because it would put firms like mine out of business."

I felt a tickle of anger. "And, as usual, business wins."

Carolina sensed my feelings and added, "There are plenty of good uses the technology can be and is being put to: identifying criminals, particularly kidnappers asking for ransom; nailing the perpetrators of frauds; discouraging nuisance callers and telemarketers."

"Then I'm all for it."

"Good. By using my firm's library, I may be able to find out who made this menacing call to you. If the person's in our catalogue, I can do it within a couple of hours. If not, I may have to go to other firms' libraries, and it'll take longer. Now, this other recording?"

"A call my office manager took, also this morning. The person never got back to me."

"Tricky, but I'll see what I can do."

4:01 p.m.

Late that afternoon I finally heard from Mrs. Kingsley, Ma's neighbor. "I've been with your mother at the hospital all day today, dear."

"Hospital? Which one? What happened?"

"She's at Monterey Peninsula Community. Now, don't go getting excited. I'm sure it's nothing serious. In fact, she asked me not to tell you, so you wouldn't rush down here and make a big fuss."

"But why is she in the hospital?"

"Well, she needed to be sedated." Mrs. Kingsley's voice had taken on an edgy note.

"Sedated? Why?"

She sighed. "I suppose you have a right to know, in spite of her wishes. There have been... episodes, both manic and depressive. She wanders off, sometimes to inappropriate places. Last week I found her in an alley, looking for your brother Joey."

"My God! He's been dead for—"

"I know, dear. I know."

"What happened this time?"

"She was in a totally manic state, making a cake for Joey's return—his favorite chocolate cake, she told me—but she let it burn and the oven did a meltdown. It's lucky there wasn't a more serious fire."

Since last Christmas, my mother had become vague and confused, but preparing for Joey's return? And now a fire?

"Do my brother and sisters know about this?"

"No. You're the only one I've told."

"Why didn't anybody from the hospital let me know?"

"Typical bureaucratic confusion. Until I got your message, I thought the doctor would notify you. He claimed I should have, and I'm sorry I didn't."

"Not your fault, Mrs. Kingsley. Nobody's, really. What's the doctor's name and number?"

"Ralph Germon." She read off the number to me.

I thanked her, told her I'd report what I found out, and ended the call. Then I sat back in my chair, closed my eyes, and breathed deeply.

When and why, I wondered, had Ma become secretive about her health?

Usually even something so small as a paper cut had sent her running for the first aid kit. And the drama at every ache and pain had been monumental. Of course, for most of her life she'd had quite an audience. But now, living alone, there was none to play to; maybe she was embarrassed at not being able to fend for herself.

Or maybe I was the only one she hadn't wanted to know, because of the off-and-on prickliness of our relationship.

I tapped on my brother John's name from my cell's contact list. Not available, leave a message. Same with sister Patsy. Charlene was living in London for the year; it was the middle of the night there. Best not to talk with her until I'd spoken with Ma's doctor.

4:47 p.m.

"I've decided," Dr. Ralph Germon said, "to tell you about your mother's condition in spite of her wishes for strict privacy. It's in her best interests for family to know what's going on."

"Her neighbor mentioned dementia."

"Dementia is a nonspecific diagnosis. Frankly, I think the relatives have more difficulty dealing with it than they do with Alzheimer's."

"Why?"

"Alzheimer's is supposedly a known disease. It has a name—although I would say we know very little about it. Dementia—well, it conjures all sorts of strange things in their minds."

"What's the prognosis of my mother's dementia?"

"Not too bad. Other than it, she's in reasonably good health. She could live for many more years."

"But the quality of her life...?"

"She is also cheerful. She tells jokes. She even... flirts a little."

That was Ma.

"And she has recently taken up knitting. Scarves, in particular."

Oh, God, "many more years" of hand-knit scarves!

"If she returns home," the doctor went on, "and I recommend she eventually does, because elderly people are most comfortable in familiar surroundings, she will need a good deal of care for a while, perhaps full-time. A nursing home—"

I blocked out what he was saying. Katie McCone in a nursing home? No way. For one thing, they'd throw her out within a week for wreaking havoc. Ma had always been a rabble-rouser.

"For now, what about family visits?"

"I don't think that's advisable. She was very emphatic that no one, especially you, know about her condition."

"Why especially me?"

"She didn't explain, but I wouldn't take it personally. The impaired mind doesn't work rationally."

You could bet I *was* going to take it personally.

Rae stuck her head through the doorway. I motioned her in.

"Doctor, I'll need to continue this discussion tomorrow. I have an important meeting now."

Rae frowned, looked around the empty office, and shrugged.

The doctor and I set a time for a next-day call, and I broke the connection.

Rae asked, "What's the matter? I take it this important meeting was an excuse to get off the phone."

I massaged my temples and explained the situation.

"That's terrible news," she said. "I barely knew my parents, and when the grandma who raised me died, I never shed a tear. She was a mean old lady. But your ma—she's special."

"I know."

"Are you going to visit her?"

"For some reason she doesn't want me to. I don't know if that extends to the rest of the family or not. I can't get hold of any of them."

Rae sat down in one of the clients' chairs. "Why would it only extend to you?"

"As you know, we haven't always had the best of relationships."

"True. What does the doctor think?"

"He mentioned a nursing home. Can you imagine Ma—"

"Jesus! No way. How long's she going to be where she's at?"

"I don't know. Medical people—they don't keep you informed on anything."

Rae looked thoughtful, twirling one of her red-gold curls around a finger. "Well, here's one solution—how about I go down there? I'm pushy enough to find out what's what. For all we know, this doc could be pimping for an expensive nursing home he owns a percentage of. That sort of self-interest does happen. You can't be too careful these days."

"I suppose you're right. The goddamn lust for profit."

Rae's offer was a relief, yet I felt conflicted. This was my mother we were talking about; I really should be the one to go to her.

I said as much, and Rae replied, "What're you going to do? Hold her hand? Besides, when family shows up, it makes too big a deal of what's going on. I can just say that Ricky's doing a concert in the area and I decided to tag along."

"But she'll know that he's not."

"I doubt she reads the arts and entertainment section of the paper. Or much of anything now."

I sighed. "Okay, you go. Tell her I'll be down to see her as soon as I can, whether she wants me to or not."

"Will do. And I'll let you know right away how she's doing."

Rae, I thought as I watched her leave, was an exceptional friend. When All Souls' budget had stretched enough for me to hire a much-needed assistant, I'd located her through a want ad. She'd looked somewhat bedraggled and unsure of herself when she came for her interview, but exuded an endearing quality that made me ask her back a second time, when I hired her on the spot. Life had not been going well for her, as she was mired in a marriage to a perpetual student who did nothing to help pay the bills. A few months of success with the co-op ended that situation, and from there on it was up and away.

By coincidence, she met my brother-in-law, country musician Ricky Savage, on the very day my sister Charlene kicked him out of her life. They began a whirlwind affair, complete with tabloid coverage, about which we all had our doubts, but what we'd said couldn't last *had* lasted. Rae proved to be a good stepmother to his six kids by Charlene; Ricky quit the philandering lifestyle that had been at the root of his difficulties with my sister; they married; and then—to all our surprise—Rae became an author. The slim suspense volume called *Blue Lonesome* led to others, and she was now firmly established in a highly competitive field.

And she still could find the time to help me out with my problems.

Bless her.

5:10 p.m.

Over the phone Carolina Owens said, "We got no recognition on the voice of the caller who hung up on your office manager, or the woman who called you at home."

"Dead end there, huh?"

"Well, yes. Frankly, from what you've told me about the missing woman, she doesn't sound like one to play those kinds of games. Do you have any recordings of her speaking at a different time and in her normal fashion? I'd like one for my files."

After a little thought, I said, "Yes. A while back she did a TV spot for the rehabbers' organization she founded. She was proud of it and gave me a copy."

"Okay, send it on over."

"Will do. Thanks, Carolina. Send me your bill."

"No bill—just give me a gallon of squid ink for my birthday."

9:30 p.m.

Dark here by the water. Cold too.

I leaned my elbows on the seawall near the Breakers and stared out at the ocean. The low-tide waves made slurring sounds as they washed against the broken sandstone and cement slabs below the wall. Fog swirled, and the horns under the bridge responded; even the rush of tires on the Great Highway was muted. The wind, growing stronger by the minute, tangled my damp hair and lifted it from my shoulders. The salt spray felt like a stinging slap to the face. I couldn't see anything except the faint phosphorescent shimmer of an occasional whitecap and the very dim lights of a freighter out in the shipping lane.

The Outerlands were a ghostly, lonely place after darkness fell. Fascination had drawn me here, but now I was in the grip of inertia. Wasn't that what Zack Kaplan had called the reason he stayed here year after year—inertia? No, he'd said "lethargy." There was a shade of difference between the two: inertia was a state of not changing; lethargy was worse—just plain laziness.

Neither was working on me now; what I felt was closer to obsession. I couldn't stay away from this place, and couldn't go forward until...

Until what?

Until I found a lead on what might have happened to Chelle here. Until I found a new direction to pursue. Until I knew what Zack had wanted to tell me.

But, no, that wasn't the whole truth. The Breakers harbored a secret that would give me an important answer to—

A door slammed somewhere behind me, and footsteps began slapping along the pavement from the north. Men, three or four from the sound of them.

They were laughing, wisecracking, having a good time. Harmless night out with the buddies.

"Whadda you get when you cross a sea lion with a bed?"

"A Sealy mattress."

"Hur-hur-hur!"

"What did the buffalo say when his son went off to college?"

"Bi-son."

"Thassa good one!"

"What's the difference between your wife and your job?"

"After five years your job will still suck."

"Woo-hoo!"

The jokes continued, each one raunchier and mostly derogatory to women.

I glanced at them as they neared me. Three—two

heavyset, one slender. Clad in ski caps and parkas and jeans. Nothing threatening about them, but, given that last joke, a harmless night out with the buddies could turn ugly...

I looked away, shifted my weight, and slid my hand into my purse, to the compartment where I keep my .38.

"Hey, there's one now!"

Oh, hell. Here we go.

Rough voice: "Hey, baby, whatcha doin' here all alone?"

Another: "You lookin' for some company, darlin'?"

I said coldly, "Good evening, gentlemen."

They kept moving toward me, close enough for one of them to put his hand on my shoulder. I removed it. The wind carried smells that made my gorge rise— whiskey and stale sweat and a curious odor that in animals of all species warns of aggression.

"Hey, it talks!" the slender one said.

"What else d'you think it might do?" the heavyset one whose nose resembled a pig's snout asked.

"Hur-hur-hur."

Oh, dammit, this is the last thing I need to deal with now!

"Yeah, what else can you do, baby?"

I took a step back.

"Hey, bitch, we're talkin' to you."

The .38 slid easily from my bag. "You want to know what else can I do?" I asked, bringing the gun out and up so they could see it. "I can shoot."

Pig snout had been about to make a grab for me. Now he froze.

"Jesus Christ," the slender one said, "she's a cop!"

Don't disabuse them of the idea.

"You want to be placed under arrest for violating Paragraph 1440, Part B of the California Penal Code? Intimidating an officer."

What I was doing was risky. I wasn't actually impersonating a cop, but it wasn't ethical behavior either. And while I've been known to dip into the penal code for occasional light reading, I had no idea if there *was* a Paragraph 1440, Part B.

The men retreated—slowly, with their hands up in front of them, the way people do when they don't want their fear to set you off.

I raised the gun higher, sighted along the barrel. And they turned tail and ran, scrambling and staggering across the Great Highway.

I didn't ease my grip on the .38. Rage boiled up, threatening to choke me.

My finger tightened on the trigger. My arms tensed, and I assumed a shooter's stance.

Then my hands started to shake.

Jesus, I almost fired after them!

Suddenly my legs went weak. I stared down at the gun. I'd carried it with me for years. Twice it had saved my life. Several times I'd used it to quell dangerous situations. And, out of necessity, I'd killed with it.

Now it felt strangely foreign in my hand.

Slowly I sank down, slid through the gap in the seawall and along the steps that gave access to the empty beach. Crumpled to the damp sand, pressed myself into a corner between the wall and the stairs. Stared at nothing.

I didn't want to think about what might have happened if things had gone bad. For a while I crouched there, shivering, not from the icy temperature but from the coldness within myself.

God, what kind of a world are we living in, where a person can so easily give in to anger and stop caring about the consequences?

TUESDAY, AUGUST 9

Restless night, dreams flowing through my subconscious.

The usual: Reenactments of previous close calls. The terror at the US/Mexican border. The plane crash in the Mojave Desert. The explosion in the mine above Tufa Lake. The frantic escape from a small Caribbean island with a nine-year-old girl whose life was at risk.

I sat up, clutching at my chest, trying to force air into my lungs. The phone rang and cats scrambled from the bed.

Hy. "Hey, McCone, I caught a ride with a pilot buddy in Amsterdam. We're at Kennedy right now, and he's taking me through to SFO with a couple of stops in between. I'll be home tonight."

"You and your worldwide buddy network. I love it."

"What's wrong?"

"Ma's in the hospital."

"Nothing serious, I hope?"

"I don't know. Rae's going down to Pacific Grove to check on her."

"You're not?"

"No, not right away. She doesn't want me there."

"Why?"

I shrugged, then realized he couldn't see me. "She wouldn't say."

"Odd. She's usually so outspoken."

"You don't have to be polite—we both know she's mouthy."

"Well, yeah. But that's not all that's bothering you. I can hear it in your voice, and I've been getting some bad vibes from you for the last couple of hours."

"Rotten dreams, that's all..."

"What kind of dreams?"

"Oh, they're only replays of how some things might've turned out if I'd...gone the other way."

"What things?"

"Oh, Ripinsky, not now. I'm muddleheaded and tired."

Pause. "My buddy's motioning me toward the plane. I'll call you back when we're airborne. I want to know what's plaguing your sleep."

"No, you don't."

"Yes, I do."

7:29 a.m.

"Okay," he said when he called again twenty minutes later. "So let's hear about those dreams."

"As I told you before, they're just replays."

"Of what?"

I explained, briefly—he'd been present at or knew about each incident.

"Common denominator?" he asked.

"Split-second life or death."

"And the outcomes?"

"Hazy. But mostly death."

"Whose?"

"Well, I'm the one dreaming them. Who do you think?" I was fully awake now and feeling testy.

"What incidents? Consider them again."

"The crack-up in the Mojave—that came out okay. And I got Habiba off Jumbie Cay. And at the mine above the lake—"

"We saved each other's lives."

"And at the border—"

"You saved my life. McCone, you went the right way every time."

"But what if these past few days I haven't? What if…?"

"Stop that! Any news about your mother?"

"No."

"Well, what's happened at the agency since we last talked?"

I told him about my case, and my near-disastrous encounter at the seawall. "I felt so out of control that it's very lucky I didn't fire on the scumbags. And you know what kind of attention that would've gotten me from the neighbors—and the cops."

"But you stopped yourself in time. You went the right way."

"But what if I'm off course now?"

"Then get off your ass and change your course. See you tonight."

7:52 a.m.

I pouted in bed for a while. Felt it was my privilege after being rebuked by my own husband. But the more I pouted, the more I felt he was right. Both about changing my course and about getting off my ass. Fortunately I had the cats to remind me to do the latter.

Alex was the larger one: male, a black shorthair with enormous paws that he used to snatch up any attractive morsel he fancied. Jessie, the female, was smaller, also black, but with a white bib and white paws that were no less effective at grabbing any article she found interesting. I once had to rescue a hummingbird from her; how she'd managed to glom onto anything so quick and alert, I'd never know.

Kibble and fresh water in the dishes. Breakfast for me: nothing. I'd had cold cereal, hot cereal, waffles, pancakes, eggs of all varieties, and toast stuffed down my throat from kindergarten to high school graduation. After I'd gone out on my own, I'd vowed to have no more of that. Yes, they say breakfast is the most important meal of the day, that your senses will be dulled and your very survival compromised without it. Well, maybe I can be a little dull at times, but considering what I do, I've survived admirably.

Take that, Post Toasties!

8:55 a.m.

Will called as I was leaving for the office. "I'm closing in on this Damon Delahanty," he said, "but he keeps moving from place to place, and it's frustrating the hell out of me."

"Which places?"

"A rental house—no, more of a shack—in Oakland. A flat in the Inner Richmond. An apartment in Daly City. Then back to the Richmond. And now—no trace of him."

"All those different places in the four years since he was released from prison?"

"He's either restless or a lousy tenant."

"E-mail me the dates and addresses for each, and keep searching. What about this Wendall Manning, the party guy on Jardin Street?"

"Parties are what he's all about: ran a store on Upper Market for twenty-seven years that rented costumes and sold balloons, invitations, funny hats, paper plates, other table decorations, even ice sculptures. I guess he must've delivered truckloads of his merchandise to the Breakers, since he called it 'a real rockin' place.'"

"Anything on Ollie Morse's records with the military?"

"Nope, nor Majewski's either, and I'm not too hopeful. You know the military…"

Yeah, I did—my father had been a career NCO in the navy.

"Nothing else to report," Will added, "but you'll hear from me as soon as I do."

9:10 a.m.

The landline rang as I was planning my day. A sales rep urging me to install some kind of fake tile over my beautiful terra-cotta kitchen floor. I cut him off in the middle of his spiel. Damn nuisance calls! Grumbling, I returned to my list.

1. Check with Rae about Ma.
2. Call Jamie Strogan and ask if he'd found anything from Missing Persons about Zack's disappearance.
3. The Curleys. I hated to tell them I had nothing positive to report, but they deserved an update.
4. Go to Rosie's Posies, where Zack worked part-time.
5. Pamela Redfin. The gregarious woman probably knew quite a bit about what was happening in the Outerlands.

Anybody else? Maybe a name would arise during my conversations.

My call to Rae was about to go to voice mail when she picked up. "All's well so far," she told me. "Your mother's still sedated, but they're gradually decreasing the dosage and will see how she responds. I've taken the liberty of moving into her place."

"You're welcome to it."

"That's what Samuel says."

"Who's Samuel?"

"Her cat."

"Ma has a cat?"

"A three-year-old tortoiseshell with an amiable disposition."

Good lord, what else didn't I know about my adoptive mother's life? "I hope you didn't find any stray boyfriends or husbands around the place."

"Not yet, but I'm still looking."

"Has Ma changed her mind about visitors?"

"She really isn't cognizant. In her lucid moments she seems more scattered and uncommunicative than yesterday."

"You think it would help if I came down there and talked to her?"

"I doubt it; it might worsen your relationship. And there's really nothing you can do."

"But I feel so helpless—"

"Rely on me, my dear."

"Thank you, I will."

Jamie Strogan had nothing to tell me, and I doubted Missing Persons would devote much time to the case. Both Chelle and Zack were of age and free to go when and where they wanted. But at least Strogan's report would be there to show I'd tried.

I couldn't reach the Curleys. My calls to both Jim's and Trish's cells weren't answered—nor did they go to voice mail. The couple hadn't checked out, Señor Engardo, the desk clerk at their hotel in Costa Rica, informed me, but there was no answer to a call to their room, and none of the staff had seen them since the previous evening. Claiming I was their daughter and asking if someone would check their room to make sure nothing was amiss there, I met with resistance until I offered to allow them to make their return call collect. In ten minutes, the desk clerk reported that all was well.

"Did you speak with either Mr. or Mrs. Curley?" I asked.

"They were not there, but all of their possessions are in place."

"Possessions. Such as...?"

"Suitcases, of course."

"Packed or unpacked?"

A muffled exchange. "Apparently they have not had time to unpack yet."

"They arrived there when?"

"Our records say yesterday morning."

"I spoke with both of them on Saturday. They had checked into your hotel and were in their room. Surely they would have unpacked then. Mrs. Curley was about to take a bath."

"I would know nothing about that, *señora*, but I can check for you."

He put down the phone. Costly minutes ticked by.

"They are not there, *señora*. Only their bags."

"Do you have a security officer there?"

"That would be I."

"And you have happened to lose two guests who checked in on Saturday, *not* Monday, and have not yet unpacked their possessions?"

"Perhaps they are out seeing the sights."

I was about to lose it. Instead I ended the conversation with him and buzzed my Spanish-speaking operative Julia Rafael. The call went to voice mail. I left her a message asking her to contact Señor Engardo and see if she could pry any more information out of him. She possessed a great deal of patience and would be better at dealing with him long-distance than I was.

Okay. Time, as Hy had told me, to get off my ass.

10:17 a.m.

The flower shop was on Irving Street, not far from
UC Med Center. Painted in attractive pastel tones on
the outside, with a light, airy interior. A center table
held vases and silk flowers; in the glass cases were various arrangements; the odor of wet earth, blossoms,
and other growing things wafted through the door of a
greenhouse at the rear.

"Help you?" a pleasant male voice called out from
beyond the door.

"I hope so."

The owner of the voice appeared: handsome, blond,
and athletically built.

"Hi, I'm Rosie. What'll it be? I've got a great price
on *Grevillea* Coastal Gem today."

"Actually, I'm looking for information—"

"I can supply that too. Soil amendment, mulches,
organic fertilizers—"

"Zack Kaplan."

His face scrunched up like a displeased child's. "You
know Zack?"

"I'm looking for him."

"So am I. What the hell's he want, for me to ransom
my own truck?"

"Your truck?"

"Yeah, mine. He makes deliveries for me. But after
he made his rounds last Saturday he never brought it
back."

"You call the police?"

"Not yet."

"Seems a long time to wait."

"I suppose. But I've known Zack since we were both students at SF State. You know how it is—a guy does you a favor, you do him a favor, and so on."

"What kinds of favors?"

"A cash loan here, a cash loan there. A place to crash on the sofa. A little lie so you don't have to hurt the wife or the girlfriend... Why're you looking at me like that? Don't you women ever do each other any favors?"

"Sure we do. I even loaned a friend my toothbrush one time."

"Yuck!" He looked seriously offended.

I took out one of my cards and handed it to him. "If you hear from Zack or he brings back your truck, will you call me?"

He glanced at it. "Oh, geez, a private eye. What'd Zack do? Rob a bank with my truck as the getaway vehicle?"

"If he had, you'd be talking with the FBI, not me."

"But what'd he *do*?"

"Nothing serious. Just call me." In the door, I paused. "How come you're called Rosie?"

"The name was on the shop when I bought it. Besides, it's better than Theophilus."

11:32 a.m.

Pamela Redfin was opening up at Danny's Inferno when I arrived. Her father hadn't come in yet.

"Anything new about Chelle?" she asked immediately.

I shook my head. "I was about to ask you the same thing."

"Not a word from or about her here."

We pulled stools to the end of the bar and sat.

Pamela said, "It's not like her to go off like this."

"No."

"Her folks must be in a real state."

"They are."

"Are they good friends of yours?"

"Yes. Former neighbors too."

"Losing a child that way..." She squeezed her eyes shut. "I know something about that."

"You mean you—?"

"No, I've never had a kid. But my mother had another daughter with her first husband. My half sister Sara was only two when she disappeared one day. They were in Golden Gate Park, and my mother took her eyes off where she was playing in a sandbox for a minute. When she looked back, no Sara. The cops never found a trace of her, and it sunk the marriage. When my mom married Dad, she told him she didn't want to have any more children. Lucky for me I was a mistake." Pamela smiled, but her eyes were melancholy. "Chelle—I bet she was wanted by her parents."

"None of the Curleys has ever spoken of that, but I suspect so."

"Are they a nice family?"

"Yes. The parents travel a lot, and it's to their credit that they don't interfere with their kids' lives. Chelle's one of the most independent women I know—but maybe their lack of parental concern is why she's had so much trouble with men."

Pamela smiled. "I thought she just had bad taste."

I considered the men Chelle had recently been with. Adam Smithson, a guy who had only used her to get at valuables he imagined were hidden in a building she was rehabbing. A wannabe musician who went into rages and smashed up his guitars, then told her to pay to replace them because "you made me mad." The stereotypical married man who swore he was going to leave his wife and two kids—"someday"—and then took the wife on a second honeymoon to Aruba.

Rather than go into all of that, I said to Pamela, "Chelle's highly spoken of here in the Outerlands."

"Everybody loves her. Since she bought that grotesque building, she's taken such an interest in the history and residents of the area."

"I know she's tight with Cap'n Bobby, but who else?"

"Me, my dad, Zack. Al, Ollie. She was especially close to Ollie; they talked a lot, most every day."

"About what?"

"I don't know. I think she was trying to help him work through this PTSD thing."

"She ever talk to you about what happened to him in Afghanistan?"

"Not to me or my dad. Chelle respects other people's privacy."

It was an admirable trait, but it sure wouldn't help my investigation.

2:11 p.m.

Julia was in her office when I came in to M&R. She'd gotten my message and spoken to Señor Engardo in

Costa Rica as I'd requested. And had better luck than I had. "I threatened him," she said, looking mighty pleased with herself.

"With what?"

"*El jefe*, the head cop in the town there. I looked his name up on the Net. He must be one tough *hombre*, because the guy at the hotel started backtracking like crazy."

"Good job." I smiled at her.

She smiled back. "Well, you gotta work the angles. You taught me that."

Julia is strong and tall, with long black hair that she wears piled atop her head. She is also very smart and a damned good operative. Her childhood on the streets of the Mission district, where her parents abandoned her at ten, had been a sordid one, and her prospects for the future had looked even worse until she located a sister who took her in when she was pregnant with her son, Tonio. The sister, and Julia's hopes for Tonio's future, had turned her life around, and by the time she answered an ad I'd placed for a Spanish-speaking operative, she had the confidence to own up to her past and describe her transformation.

"So what did you find out?"

The smile turned into a frown. "It was all a 'big misunderstanding.' The Curleys arrived, as you said, late Saturday afternoon. They had dinner in the hotel's cantina, then went out on the town. While they were out, there were two calls for them from a San Francisco number, no message." She held out a piece of notepaper.

The number wasn't a familiar one.

When I looked questioningly at her, she said, "It's

new, maybe unlisted. I've got a friend at the phone company working on whose it is. You said you spoke to both of the Curleys on Saturday?"

"In the late evening, yes."

"You sure it was both of them?"

"I'm sure."

"Uh-huh. The desk clerk tried to convince me that only one of them returned from their Friday night on the town. I asked him, why was my employer able to speak with both of them on Saturday? Why are there now still two unpacked suitcases in the room?"

"And he said?"

"Well, he kind of ran out of his *Español.* His *Ingles* too. He babbled, he cursed—in both languages—and then he hung up on me. The phone at the hotel has been out of commission ever since."

"My God, we've got to do something!"

"It's under way." She grinned widely. "By now *el jefe*, Jaime Estenzione, who seems to be a very cooperative individual, is questioning Señor Engardo and will let us know as soon as he gets the answers we need."

4:39 p.m.

Tense time waiting. I attended to some paperwork, grew bored with it, and gave up. I collected Julia and we climbed up to the roof garden, where we shared some wine.

The ever-present August fog was creeping over the towers of the Golden Gate on a trajectory that I knew would eventually envelop AT&T Park. Was there a baseball game scheduled for tonight? Didn't matter; the team had tanked, with too little time left in the schedule to get back on its feet. Most fans would take the weather as a welcome invitation to stay home.

"You know," Julia said, "Chelle, she seems to be a pretty good kid. Would she have run off to be in Costa Rica with her parents and not called them first?"

"No. And I doubt she's in Costa Rica. Helene in the research department says there's no record of her entering the country."

"You said she took her cell and laptop with her."

"She—or somebody else—did. According to Helene, she hasn't used them since."

"A kidnapping, you think?"

"Possibly. Chelle's tough, but somewhat naïve."

"And the parents? Could they have been kidnapped too?"

I shook my head. "I don't see any reason they would have been. They're not wealthy."

"Then where are they?"

"That I don't understand at all."

Julia's cell rang. After a moment she mouthed at me, "Local call. My phone company friend."

I waited.

"Yeah? You're kidding. Really. Thanks, I owe you." She clicked off, then turned to me. "Well, surprise!"

"What?"

"The SF number that someone called the Curleys from is a brand-new one, belonging to your buddy Hank Zahn."

Hank. My best male friend, going all the way back to college. Partner, along with his wife Anne-Marie Altman, in the best family law practice in the city.

Trish and Jim must've decided they needed an attorney. Well, they were in good hands.

Julia's phone rang again. Costa Rica, finally. "Si, Señor Estenzione...No...? *Y Señor Engardo...? Sí, comprendo... Bueno.*"

She sighed as she replaced the phone in her jacket pocket. "The desk clerk told Chief Estenzione that the Curleys had requested a room change—the reason their bags were in the new room unpacked. The desk clerk is now being 'rigorously interrogated' by the authorities—poor bastard."

I couldn't feel for the lying desk clerk, but I feared for the Curleys. I'd never been to Costa Rica, but I remembered the terror of the last time I'd worked a case in Mexico and had been lied to, scammed, and ultimately flown over the jungle by a pilot intent on pushing me out over the deep-green canopy below.

"Shar?"

"I've got to call Hank. Maybe he knows... something."

5:27 p.m.

The phone rang at least seven times at the new number Hank had left with the desk clerk at the Curleys' hotel in Costa Rica. Then it was picked up and I heard, "Hell! Shit! Why doesn't this machine work?"

In spite of my tension, I had to smile. Hank is the world's most inept person at dealing with technology—even simple tech.

I said, "I think you have to turn it on first."

"That might be the problem. Damn answering machine." Clicking noises, a dropped receiver, a couple more curses, and then a sigh. "All right—here I am."

"What's with the new number?"

"I'll go into that later. What can I do for you?"

Very abrupt, very unlike Hank.

"I understand you've been leaving messages for Trish and Jim Curley in Costa Rica."

"Uh, yeah. But I can't reach them."

"Neither can I. Have they retained you? For what? And don't give me any of your client confidentiality crap."

Pause. I couldn't tell if he was considering my request or still fiddling with the recalcitrant machine.

After a moment he said, "No money's changed hands, but I consider myself retained."

"To do what?"

"You know I can't—"

"Okay, let me tell you: the Curleys' daughter Chelle has vanished; they've asked me to look for her. I think they've retained you to protect her legal status."

"Why would they?"

"That I don't know. But look at it this way: She's disappeared and the SFPD is being extremely casual about investigating it. Wouldn't you seek counsel if it were your daughter who'd disappeared?"

Silence.

I asked, "Have I compromised your legal ethics in any way?"

"Of course not, but I sure hate it when you've gotten way ahead of my thinking."

"Anything they told you that could help me deal with the situation?"

"They're a closemouthed couple. There's a reserve about them that I can't get past even when we're talking about their own daughter."

"Then we'll have to wait out their silence. Now, what's with you?"

"Oh, Shar, please don't ask me now."

But I already knew: a new phone number; a new answering machine; the hollowness in his voice. He and Anne-Marie had split up.

I've seen it again and again, as we approach this middle stage of our lives: *Something's missing. This isn't the deal I signed up for. I'm tired of the same old life.*

I said, "I'm not going to ask you anything you don't want to talk about. Except where are you?"

"New apartment, a couple of floors down from your brother John and three floors up from Mick. New home. I mean I guess it's home." Pause, then heavily, "She...just walked out. I couldn't stay there in the house we shared."

"Where's Habiba?" Their adopted daughter, whom I'd rescued from an abusive family on a remote Caribbean island.

"In her bedroom in Anne-Marie's apartment."

Anne-Marie and Hank were—had been—one of those couples who couldn't live together—neat freak and slob—but for years they'd coexisted very well in a two-flat house in the Noe Valley district. Until now.

"How's she taking the breakup?"

"Quietly. You know her: so much disruption and deception in her life. I'm not sure it's too good that she's learned to handle it in silence."

Maybe, maybe not.

I asked, "Would it help if I talked to her?"

"Definitely. You're her hero. She often reminds us of how the two of you took your 'big swim.'"

"I'll call her, then. We can reminisce about the big swim."

"Thanks, Shar. Love you. But about the Curleys—"

"Don't worry about them. I've decided to send someone who speaks the language to locate them."

6:10 p.m.

"I'll be glad to go," Julia said when I explained what I wanted her to do.

"Good. Leave for Costa Rica as soon as possible."

"First flight out."

I hadn't asked her any of the crap questions too often fired at women when they're asked to travel for business purposes: *Will your husband mind? Will the kids be okay? Have you put up enough casseroles so the family won't starve? Has the laundry been done for the week? Are you sure you won't mind being all on your lonesome?*

Of course most of them didn't apply to Julia's situation: she had no husband; she had only one precociously independent son who went to a great school three blocks from home; her sister took excellent care of the household duties; and Julia was never lonely in a strange place, because she wasn't shy about striking up conversations with interesting people she met.

"I'll be in touch when I have anything to report," she said.

"Vaya con Dios."

7:20 p.m.

I moved from my desk to the armchair under Mr.
T. and stared out at the lights of Marin. Mr. T. was
my schefflera tree, named in honor of Ted, who had
procured him from the Flower Mart. Darkness was
gathering quickly, and I thought of the nights in
mid-November, when we would go off daylight saving. Initially those nights were always grim, but they
brightened when the holiday lights appeared. For
the last two weeks in December, the dark seemed
a cozy blanket wrapped around the season's events.
But then came January, February, and March: either
cold and rainy or hot and parched. Nobody can
predict the weather patterns now, and I've given up
trying.

A call from Rae brightened my mood.

"Your mother was a little more scattered than usual
today," she said, "but cheerful and pleasant. She gifted
me with a scarf she made."

I breathed out a sigh of relief, balancing the phone
receiver between my shoulder and my ear.

"I was right about the doc," Rae went on. "He's
shilling for a very expensive nursing home. I'm looking
into home care for her."

"How did I get a friend like you?"

"Lucky, I guess."

"Did you tell her I'll visit her soon?"

"Yep. She says for you not to bother. And not to
worry so much about her, she'll be fine."

"That's what she always says. A good sign."

"I thought so too." Rae paused, then chuckled.

"Wait until you see the scarf. Purple with little yellow dots. Maybe I should pass it on to Ted. It'd go well with one of those Botany 500 jackets of his."

"Good idea."

When we ended the call, I was smiling—for the first time that day.

8:44 p.m.

"Hey, Shar," Habiba said when I called her cell. "What's up?"

"I'd like to hire you as an expert witness for one of my investigations."

"How much you paying?"

"Two slices of pizza at Gina's."

"Cool."

"And a Coke."

"This one must be a biggie."

"Yes, it is. Remember when you told me during our big swim how desperately you wanted to escape that island where your dad was holding you?"

"Not something I'm ever gonna forget."

"Well, what if you were in trouble here in the city and wanted to get away without anybody knowing—where would you go?"

"Why would I? I love it here, and I love Anne-Marie and Hank—both of them, in spite of the breakup. Do you know—?"

"We'll talk about that in a minute. But for now, considering you're older and more mobile than you were in the Caribbean, how would you manage it?"

"Ummm...Let me think." Long pause. "Would I have a car?"

"No." Chelle owned a truck, but it had broken down, so she had been borrowing from friends while saving for a new one.

"Would I have a friend who would lend me one?"

"Probably not for a very long time."

"Not even a boyfriend?"

"Not even." Except for the swinish one Chelle had recently booted out of her life.

"Okay," Habiba said, "that means public transit. Not great or fast, but easy to hide on. Nobody ever looks at you on a bus or a train or even on a plane. You'd have to wear a weird costume or do something gross to make them turn their heads. One time this drunk guy threw up on my foot on Muni. It was awful, and everybody was horrified, but the driver refunded my fare."

That I didn't need more detail on.

"You wouldn't hitchhike?"

"Not with all the weirdos on the road."

"Bicycle?"

"If you want to go any distance, they're too slow, and even if you lock one up, it's likely to get stolen."

"How else, then?"

"Well, there *is* one way, but if you ever tell Hank or Anne-Marie I know about it, I'll unfriend you."

To her cybergeneration, the most dire threat in the universe. Even though I don't use any of the social networks, I said, "I promise."

"Okay. There's this guy named Billy Clyde who runs a company called the Young Freedom Line. Cheap fares and no questions asked, to other cities and dif-

ferent airports. Most of the kids who use it are trying
to escape their homes. My friend Ursula, her mother
was dead and her father beat on her something bad.
She took the bus and sent me a postcard from Denver.
Just the one, saying the trip was fine and she was happy
there. I never heard from her again, though."

Habiba's voice was sad and reflective. She was
thinking similar things as I: the bus had dropped off its
young and naïve riders in a bad neighborhood; without much money, both the girls and the boys had been
dragged down into a human cesspool; even the ones
who were able to send a postcard to a friend back
home had probably not survived the undertow.

"Okay," she said, "about the breakup…"

"Yes. What happened?"

"Not all that much at first. They just kind of
stopped being together or talking with each other. It
was like she'd be up here and he'd be down there, but
they didn't visit back and forth, and the three of us
never had dinners or watched TV together, or went out
anyplace. Then, the other night, she came downstairs
with her suitcases all packed. She travels a lot for business and I knew she had a trip scheduled for Chicago,
so I didn't think much of it. But then he asked me to
go to my room, and I did, and they started in on each
other."

"You didn't happen to hear any of it?" I asked.

"Well, it's hard *not* to hear anything in this house."

"Especially when you know all the places to listen
in from."

"Okay, my ears were flapping."

"What did they say?"

"He asked her to stay. She said no. He asked her

why she was leaving. She said she couldn't believe how thick he was. He said she should tell him why he was 'so thick.' She told him all the life had gone out of their relationship, the comradeship, the adventure. I kind of cringed, thinking it was maybe because of me, a kid weighing them down. But then she said, 'The best memories I'm taking away from here are our times with Habiba.' And she left."

I felt hollow inside. The things we do to our children... And the things we do to one another...

Habiba said, "I can't talk about this any more."

"I understand."

"Shar, I won't lose you too, will I?"

"I'll always be here for you, my big swimmer."

She sighed, a little contented sound, and broke the connection.

WEDNESDAY, AUGUST 10

7:35 a.m.

A great day to be alive. The sun was shining, and through the bedroom windows that faced the backyard I heard mourning doves cooing. A lot of people think they're creepy, but I find their gentle sounds soothing. To me, if they're out in their nest in our apple tree, it's a sign that things will go right during the coming day.

I looked over at Hy. He was deeply asleep, his arms wrapped around an oversize pillow as they'd been wrapped around me last night. After I came home, I'd been surprised that he wasn't already there, but he appeared an hour later while I was curled up on the couch reviewing files that I'd neglected all week because of my concern for Chelle.

"Stuck in a holding pattern at SFO," he said, stopping to pat Alex, who had run downstairs when he heard Hy's car pull into the garage. "Flight ahead of mine was at the five hundred level on twenty-eight R when a drone almost clipped its nose. I was in the cockpit of my flight—first officer is a buddy of mine, let me sit in—and I tell you, it was scary even from there."

I let the files slide to the floor and went to hug him. "Something's got to be done about those drones."

"I'll say." He kissed me, then held me tight, smoothing back my hair. "The FAA's trying to work on the problem, but"—he sighed—"you know bureaucracy."

Now, as I watched him sleep, I considered how much danger was factored into our combined lives. Any case could end badly. Any flight in our plane too. And then I thought of other people who went about their days quietly, who had no intimation of disaster until it struck: the secretary exiting her cubicle just before a berserk coworker ran down the aisle with a semiautomatic weapon; a crowd crossing the street when a drugged-up driver appeared out of nowhere and mowed them down; people praying in their church when a disaffected, crazed parishioner opened fire.

The world was getting edgier, scarier; good sense had been eroded; since the last election day, megalomania had spread like the Black Plague.

It no longer seemed like such a great day to be alive.

And then the phone rang. Alex levitated from my feet. Jessie stuffed her head under Hy's pillow. Hy moaned and made a make-it-go-away gesture. I picked up.

Chelle's voice said, "Hi, Sharon, it's me."

Only it wasn't Chelle's voice. Close to, but clearly an imitation.

What the hell was this? The only way to find out was to play along with the caller's game.

"Where have you been?" I demanded.

"I had to get away."

"Why?"

"Damon. He was terrorizing me."

"How?"

"Geez, Sharon, you sound so hard."

"Geez": she never used that expression. And "Sharon": she always called me Shar.

"Where are you?" I asked.

"I can't tell you that."

"Why not?"

"I'm scared they'll kill me if I do!"

The melodramatic pitch of her voice made me want to laugh.

"Who are 'they'?"

"I can't tell you. Please, Sharon, I need money!"

"How much?"

"Five thousand in cash."

As if I would simply supply that amount without question. "Why? What for?"

"I said I'm afraid they'll kill me if I don't pay them!"

Bullshit. I hit the Disconnect button.

The bogus Chelle didn't call back.

Fortunately, in our house, we have a highly sophisticated phone system, designed by my nephew Mick and his fellow operative Derek Frye. It records all incoming calls, whether we answer them or not; forwards them to our other devices; provides information on the numbers where the calls originated and the owners of the numbers, if available; records all calls we originate; keeps logs; provides call frequency and percentages and mostly useless other data. It doesn't have voice identification yet, but I'd told Carolina Owens I'd like to have her set it up.

The fake call from Chelle had originated from a number in the 916 area code—Sacramento. When I dialed it, a machine answered, "Capitol City Café," and went on to describe the menu, which didn't sound too appetizing.

I logged on to the Internet and looked up the café. Nothing about it indicated any possible connection with Chelle. I couldn't recall an instance in which any of the Curleys had mentioned Sacramento—except to bitch about our state government.

At nine o'clock I reached Carolina Owens at her office and played the recording for her to copy for testing. She got back to me within the hour.

"It was definitely not your girl," she said. "For one thing, it originated from a landline, unlike a cellular unit like the earlier recording you brought to me; those are the most difficult to pin down. I can tell you much more detail about this one: The speaker's not one of the pros who make these kind of calls for a living. She's trying too hard to control the tension in her voice. Breathing's off too—again, nervousness. I'd put her in her midtwenties, and because of the little puffs between some of her words, I'd say she's a smoker. There're some barely detectable background noises— could be somebody prompting her on what to say, or maybe just traffic. If they are traffic noises, she was pretty high above street level."

I wrote down, "Sacto/high traffic/tall building."

"That's good information," I said.

"We aim to please."

Next I placed a call to Eric Lopez, owner of a Sacramento agency that sometimes took on work for us.

"Capitol City Café?" he said. "Sure I know it. It's the rooftop restaurant of the Twenty-First Century Grand Hotel on N Street."

"A woman there placed a threatening call to me this morning."

"Not good. I assume your phone system picked up on the exact number?"

"It was the general number, the one that recites the menu."

"Uh-huh. What time did the call come in?"

"Seven thirty-five."

"Too early for anybody but staff to be in; they don't open till noon. Give me a while, and I'll get back to you."

I was puzzled and worried. Chelle's disappearance had originally seemed a case of a parent's or a young person's lack of communication. Now, with the bogus call from Sacramento, the situation felt ominous. The ransom demand made me wonder what kind of people had latched on to the case in the hope of profit.

Time to get moving. I decided to first look up Billy Clyde, the man Habiba had told me about.

11:30 a.m.

Billy Clyde was an emphatic talker and a spitter. Each pronunciation he made was accompanied by a fine spray of saliva that made me edge back from him. If he continued in this manner, I'd eventually end up three city blocks away. His appearance wasn't too good either: wild blond hair that stuck out in all directions; a mustache that had grown too long and kept getting into his mouth; crazed electric-blue eyes that hinted at substance abuse.

I'd been surprised to reach him this early at his office in the Young Freedom Line garage on Folsom Street near Bernal Heights. When I asked if we could talk about the buses he said sure, we could talk, but not on the phone. "They're all tapped," he added.

"They are? By whom?"

"Them. You know—*them*."

Oh, Lord, I was dealing with a paranoiac.

"You come here," he told me.

I couldn't resist feeding his paranoia. "How do you know your office isn't bugged?"

"It isn't. I guarantee it."

He sounded like a television huckster trying to sell me a deal on a bad used car.

The garage was cavernous, its concrete floor stained and oil slicked; a battered Toyota was pulled up near the corner that was glassed off as an office. The only other vehicle was a panel truck that might seat ten people max. No identifying logo on it, but then why would you want to advertise that you were aiding young people who wanted to escape their lives?

I showed Billy Clyde Chelle's picture and he nodded. "Not likely I'd forget her. She wanted to go to SFO last Saturday. Or was it Sunday? Don't remember, but it doesn't matter 'cause she didn't get there. She asked me to take the long way around, on Evans Avenue, on account of she had a friend near there who might loan her some money. But when we crossed Nelson Street she yelled for me to pull over. Got out of the bus and ran."

"Ran where?"

"Right on Nelson."

I pictured the neighborhood: it is close to the

former naval shipyard, and there's not a lot there, just boatyards and marine supply firms, with modest dwellings scattered in between. But if Chelle had a friend there, why had she taken Billy Clyde's shuttle to the airport? Why not a regular bus or cab? Or why not call the friend and ask her to meet her someplace? Something wrong, maybe with Billy Clyde's story?

"She have any luggage with her?" I asked.

"Just one of those backpacks like they all carry."

"Did she say anything to you?"

"Not a word till she yelled for me to stop."

"Okay, Mr. Clyde. Thanks for the information. By the way, does your bus line extend to places like Reno or Utah or Denver?"

"Sure does. Where the kids wanna go, we take them."

"Hmmm. Do you know the federal statutes about transporting minors across state lines?"

"Aaah, that." He waved his hand in negation. "Nobody's gonna bother ol' Billy Clyde about that. The kids love me."

"Do the parents love you too?"

He scowled at me, transforming his face into a badly carved jack-o'-lantern.

"You might consider getting into another line of work," I added.

He bristled, jowls shaking.

I left, having given him something to think about.

1:10 p.m.

Next I took myself off to Nelson Street, where Chelle
had exited Billy Clyde's van.

The weather, at least in this part of town, had
turned gray and misty. Few people were out and about
on the sidewalks, and those who were carried furled
umbrellas against the possible rain. Rain, I thought ir-
ritably as I parked my car in one of the few curbside
spaces. Rain in August when we had badly needed it
in February and March. But they say there's no such
thing as climate change. No, sir!

I didn't have an umbrella, but then I seldom carry
one. They distract me, and I'm in entirely too much
danger of poking a fellow pedestrian in the eye with
one of the spokes. A well-insulated hoodie usually
gives me as much protection as I need, and if it doesn't,
well, I'm washable.

I walked along, surveying the residential part of the
neighborhood. Most of the homes were two- or three-
story boxes with eyelike windows on the second and
third floors and street-level entries and garages. Most
of the entries were protected by security grilles. On a
day like today, their pastel colors looked washed out,
in need of refreshing. A couple of small corner stores
anchored the few blocks.

I decided to start with the stores.

No one at the N Street Market recognized my photo
of Chelle. The proprietor of Gordo's Groceries
thought he'd seen her around the neighborhood, but
he couldn't remember when. After that I started a
house-to-house canvass.

Ofelia Wilson: "Cute kid, looks sorta like my son's girlfriend. But, no, I ain't seen her."

George Rodriguez: "She doesn't look like anybody from around here, does she, Lanie?" His wife, Lanie: "Well, no. But these kids, they all look alike—grungy."

Ruth Chang: "I don't recognize her, but you might try up the street at Ginny London's house—the one with the stone lions on the steps. Ginny's young—only in her twenties. Inherited the place from her mother, who died last year. She gets a lot of young visitors."

Ginny London smiled at me when she opened her door and I handed my card to her. Then she covered her mouth briefly to conceal two missing front teeth.

"You're Chelle's friend. Come in, please."

I followed her along a dark hallway that opened into a sitting room; large, brightly colored cushions were scattered over its huge Oriental carpet. "She's talked a lot about you," she added, motioning for me to sit. "You're kind of her hero."

I just hoped Chelle wasn't off playing the kind of games that had made me her hero.

Ginny offered refreshments, which I refused, then sat down on a purple corduroy cushion across from the crimson velvet one I'd chosen.

"Have you seen Chelle lately?" I asked.

"Sure. Just the other day." She frowned. "She dropped by, in a big hurry. Needed to borrow some money."

"How much?"

"Two hundred. Sounds like not much, but I didn't have it." She smiled again, not bothering to conceal the gap in her mouth. "I got a big settlement from the asshole who did this to me, but I already spent it."

"What happened?"

"Fight at Pacific Rollers—that's a rink a few blocks away from here. This guy didn't think I was traveling fast enough, so he punched me out."

I'd heard roller-skating and derbies were on the way back, but I hadn't realized the sport could get so violent. I'd never been to a match, and now I definitely never wanted to go to one.

"Does Chelle skate?" I asked.

"Hell no. All she does is work. Girl's gonna be a billionaire before she's thirty."

"Did she tell you why she needed the two hundred?"

"No, and I didn't ask. Her business." Ginny frowned, finally catching the drift of my questions. "Hey, what's the problem? Is Chelle okay?"

"She's fine," I said to forestall a long conversation. "Did she say where she was going when she left here?"

"Home. She thought she'd be safe there till she could raise some cash."

"Safe from who? Or what?"

"Again, I didn't ask. The way that girl looked, she was plenty scared. In case somebody came around looking for her, I thought it wouldn't be good for me to have answers to their questions. Besides, she's probably just on vacation."

"On vacation? Wasn't she just on vacation a while ago, back East someplace?"

"Yes. I guess she liked it so much she went back. That is one traveling family. Costa Rica, Peru, Brazil— they never stop. The money they spend, but Chelle couldn't even get her hands on two hundred."

"Tell me, if you were going to SFO, what public transit would get you there fastest?"

Ginny didn't notice the abrupt change of subject. "The Muni to SamTrans. That's the way I always go, anyway."

"Well, thanks, Ginny. I'll catch up with Chelle sooner or later." I left my card with her and headed back to the agency.

2:41 p.m.

Later, in my office, I sat doodling on a legal pad. The Muni and San Mateo County Transit routes that Chelle might have caught to SFO weren't going to be of use to me. Drivers' schedules switch and, given the number of faces they see on a given day, no one is memorable to them unless it's Elvis risen from the dead.

Then there was the problem of the airlines—with thirty-some of them making multiple departures every day, where do you start? If I could narrow it down to a few flights, I had an informant at the FAA who would provide me with passenger lists, but the question was, which ones? I had no proof that Chelle had gone to Costa Rica. Did she have relatives elsewhere in this country? Maybe relatives whom her parents might be visiting? That would explain why they were gone. Did Chelle have a passport? Yes, the family had spent a couple of weeks in Spain last year.

The phone rang and I picked up without waiting for any of my employees to do so. Julia's voice said, "*Es muy buena en Costa Rica.*"

"Are you at the hotel?"

"*Sí. Es muy elegante.* These Curley friends of yours sure know how to travel." Then her tone became serious. "They aren't here, though. Señor Engardo, the desk clerk who checked them in, has been fired. The new desk clerk knows nothing. Their suitcases have vanished—someone came to pick them up, the clerk claims. Who? I asked. He didn't know the man, but he had a release form. Where was that form now? Who knows? I hate these Latino runarounds."

"You'd get the same in Paris, Tokyo, or Cape Town. When people have something to hide, or have been paid to, they'll come up with any number of lame excuses."

"I guess so. Anyway"—her tone brightened—"I'm now going out to familiarize myself with the town. Maybe I'll find out something by accident."

Probably not. I could picture her seated at a sidewalk café, drinking a mojito and enjoying the sunshine. She deserved the respite; Julia worked long, hard hours and was a damned good operative.

The door to my office, where I'd been hiding to think the case through, opened, and a familiar voice called out, "I'm home, matey!"

Mick, back from Australia.

I got up from my chair and enveloped him in a big hug. He hugged me back. "Why do I have the feeling that this welcome indicates I'm badly needed here?"

"You are, matey," I told him.

4:55 p.m.

"So that's what's been going on," I said to Mick. We were at a sidewalk table at Angie's Deli, drinking wine and eating nachos. I'd first told him about Ma, then everything about Chelle's disappearance.

Mick's face scrunched in thought. He looked good—tanned, his blond hair longish and sun streaked; the deep lines around his eyes that I'd noticed before his vacation had softened. Those lines had been caused by a combination of disappointments and out-right catastrophes. Early last year his longtime live-in partner Alison had left him—and left the house they'd been restoring on Potrero Hill feeling empty and cold. Next, just before Christmas, the house had been vandalized by a group of white supremacists—an action directed at me, but they were too stupid to get the address right. Finally, in April, he and Derek Frye had lost potential funding for a project that, as they put it, would "set the tech industry on its ear."

But now Mick looked as if he'd put all that behind him.

"Chelle," he said. "I can't believe she's gotten herself into such a mess. Or her parents."

"What's your take on it?"

"Well, there's the extortion ploy. The Curleys—do they have money? I mean, they travel a lot."

"They travel on cut-rate tickets and deals at hotels."

"What about Chelle?"

"Strictly hand-to-mouth. She urges owners of run-down properties to sell cheap, gets bank loans cosigned by her parents, begs long escrow periods from people."

"Does she deliver on her promises?"

"So far as I know, yes."

"What bank does she deal with?"

"Bank of America, I think."

"D'you know if she has a passport?"

"My guess is she does."

"Well, that's all recoverable information. The Curleys give you permission to search their house?"

"By the time I thought of that, they'd vanished."

He rubbed his chin. "We could go to the cops, try to convince them that they have probable cause—but they might not believe us, and even if they did, they'd be the ones doing the searching, without knowing what they were looking for."

"Do *we* know?"

"No. But if we found it, we'd recognize it."

I caught his drift.

"How's the Church Street neighborhood these days?" he asked.

"Quiet. I sold the lot where my old house was to a guy who wants to build condos on it, but he lost most of his money on a bad investment last spring. The Halls—on the other side—spend most of their time in Lake Havasu City."

"That's where they moved London Bridge to, isn't it?"

"Yes."

"What a travesty. Okay—the three houses across the street?"

"I don't know anybody who lives in them now, and they don't know me."

"Okay, how about having an on-site look? How're you about that?"

I frowned. "What d'you mean?"

"Are you ready and willing to break and enter the Curley house once the sun goes down?"

I smiled. "It won't be B&E—I have a key to the house. Have had it for years."

6:55 p.m.

It wasn't full dark yet, but the tail end of Church Street, beyond where the streetcar tracks turn and stop, was quiet. A couple of dogs barked and a child wailed in the distance and an ambulance screamed from over at St. Luke's Hospital, but otherwise it felt like the country on a fine August night. We parked in front of the weedy lot where my house once had stood, and memories flooded me.

An earthquake cottage, hastily and shabbily built to house homeless families after the great quake of 1906. Originally two rooms, designed to give no more than shelter, then enlarged by a later owner to include a rudimentary kitchen. Finally the back porch and an indoor toilet had been added. By my own labor and with the aid of inexpensive—and often inept— contractors, I'd transformed it. Lived there happily until an ex-con former client decided to burn it down. Even now, I could remember the choking smoke, the charring heat.

I turned my eyes away, focused on the Curley house. It was a bungalow, aluminum sided and painted a grayish blue. Its front steps rose steeply from the sidewalk. I motioned to Mick to follow and mounted them, automatically reached into the mailbox. Nothing. Trish and Jim must have stopped their deliveries when traveling. I fitted the key that they'd given me years ago into the lock; it turned smoothly.

The foyer inside was totally dark. I fumbled around for the light switch, but Mick found it first. The bulb that came on was faint, and I hesitated, getting my bearings.

A short hallway bypassed two bedrooms and a bathroom and ended in a kitchen and dining area that stretched the width of the house. Beyond was an equally wide family room and beyond that a deck. I went through the kitchen and family room and flicked on the deck lights—nothing out there but an astonished raccoon.

Mick met up with me in the family room. It was, as always, well used. This was a very laid-back household. Newspapers and magazines were stacked on the end tables; the big screen of the TV was smudged by fingerprints; shoes had been kicked off on the floor; a pair of used wineglasses sat on the coffee table in front of the couch. I closed my eyes, picturing the room as it always had been over the years. No significant changes.

Back to the kitchen, Mick following. Yes, a *very* relaxed household. A couple of dishes floated in the sink, covered in soap-and-grease scum. The garbage can reeked. I didn't remember Trish and Jim as being such careless people.

Mick asked, "Is it possible Chelle was eating some of her meals here and skimped on the cleanup? Doesn't seem like she'd leave such a mess."

"No, she's pretty fastidious."

"Doesn't seem like the Curleys would leave it like this either. Unless they were in a hurry."

"I'm sure they wouldn't." I was looking around for other inconsistencies, and found them: butter congealing in a dish on the cutting board; a jar of jam with its lid off; a loaf of bread covered in mold. "This is not right," I added.

I went to the utility closet between the kitchen and family rooms. Found mildewed towels in the washer.

"Somebody's been staying here," I said.

Mick didn't reply. He was standing at a side window off the dining room.

"Shar, come here."

I went over and looked around him. The glass was shattered, and a space large enough for a medium-size person to crawl through had been cleared of the shards of glass. "Whoever broke in," I said, "it wasn't Chelle."

"But she could have been staying here when somebody broke in."

"Just what I was thinking."

"I'll call the cops."

"No, not yet."

I backtracked along the hall to the front door and began examining the individual rooms, looking for anything that was misplaced or gone.

Everything—knickknacks, books, sofa pillows, vases, sound equipment, and TVs—was in its proper place. Of course, a lot might have changed here since I'd really taken a close look at my friends' home, but the sameness told me the broken window didn't signify robbery or vandalism.

I sank down onto a chair at the built-in desk in the kitchen. A drawer had been left slightly open, a small corner of paper poking out. Before I opened it I pulled on a pair of the thin rubber gloves I keep in my bag.

Inside was a jumble of papers, writing implements, and old check registers.

"Shar—?" Mick said.

I stood up. "I've got one more place to check out. In the meantime, please find a big plastic bag and dump the contents of this drawer into it."

Off the kitchen there was a door that led to a narrow stairway to the space under the house. Not a basement exactly, but a place that harbored a furnace and water heater. Behind the furnace was a coal chute that had seldom been used, since most San Francisco houses had been converted to gas long ago. A plywood sheet blocked the entrance to it; I pulled it aside and shone my flash into the chute.

Yes, that was what I'd expected. A few blankets and a rumpled pillow lay in the small space, an empty plastic bottle of spring water beside them. The faint scent of Chelle's sandalwood perfume clung to them. She'd been hiding here, for how long I couldn't tell.

"Shar?" Mick called from upstairs.

"Come down here!"

He appeared as I came out from behind the furnace. "This is where Chelle was holed up?"

"She must've been scared to death of somebody, poor kid. The same person who broke in, probably."

"D'you suppose whoever it was grabbed her?"

"Or scared her off, and she ran. The question is, where is she now?"

"That's not the only question."

No, it wasn't. The most important one was: Was she still alive?

10:55 p.m.

The last place I'd expected to spend my late evening was the city morgue.

The phone call I'd received on my way home from the Curley house had made me turn around and head straight to Zuckerberg SF General Hospital. The morgue, which had been relocated to the second story of the hospital in July of 2016, is brightly lit and pleasant; you experience none of the gloomy, cold clamminess of the old location. Furnishings are comfortable, private viewing rooms are discreet. A totally different experience for those of us who'd had reason to visit the old morgue.

The call had been from Jamie Strogan. The ME's office had received a male body found in an overgrown lot in the Outer Richmond; they'd cross-referenced his identification to my report and needed me to confirm it. "We've been unable to locate his next of kin," Jamie had added.

When I arrived at the morgue, Jamie and another homicide inspector, Robert Cooksen, met me in the reception room. Cooksen fit right in there: with his narrow face, thin lips, and trim black suit, he could have been a visiting mortician. He acknowledged Jamie's introduction with a grunt and turned away to confer with an attendant. Then we went into a small room with a viewing screen.

The body shown on the screen was indeed Zack Kaplan, and I said so. I'd prepared myself for this, but the sight of him still made me wince. His skin was very pale, verging on blue, his features waxen. In many ways he'd been like a big kid, with his curiosity about and passion for the detecting business. I'd sensed he didn't have a mean bone in his body—and this was what it had gotten him.

"How was he killed?" I asked Jamie.

"Stabbed in the stomach."

Above the sheet they'd draped over the fatal wound, I could make out another, oddly shaped lesion. "That doesn't look like a stab wound on his shoulder."

"It's not. We suspect it's some kind of gang signature."

"He wasn't a gang member." There'd been no mention of any affiliation in the backgrounding Will Camphouse had done on him.

Cooksen motioned to the technician inside and pointed out the wound. "Let's take a closer look at that," he said.

The marking was reasonably fresh: three concentric circles around a dot. Something that resembled an arrow pierced the circles, upper right to lower left. The carved symbol stood out in stark relief against his white skin. The more I looked at it, the more familiar it seemed.

I'd seen something like that recently. But where?

"So, Ms. McCone," Cooksen said, "have you any information that may shed light on what happened to the deceased?"

There was something about the inspector that I didn't like. His raised eyebrows and the twist of his mouth were condescending. I glanced at Jamie; he shrugged, but I had the feeling he shared my opinion of Cooksen.

"Mr. Kaplan called me sometime after ten p.m. on

Saturday, August sixth," I said, "and asked me to meet with him at his home, apartment five in the Breakers on Jardin Street. When I arrived there, he was gone."

"Why did he wish to see you?"

"He didn't say, specifically."

"Yet you went anyway."

"From what he did say, I assumed he had information on a missing person case I'm working." I told him of Chelle's disappearance, referred him to Cap'n Bobby. Then I asked, "When was Mr. Kaplan killed?"

Jamie replied. "From what the preliminary coroner's report tells us, he's been dead since late Saturday. Possibly killed somewhere else and his body dumped in high weeds in that vacant lot. A dog walker taking a shortcut through the lot stumbled over it, literally."

Cooksen asked, "Are you sure you don't know why Mr. Kaplan needed to urgently talk with you?"

"I didn't say it was urgent, Inspector."

"The lateness of the hour..."

"Don't you ever get calls at ten p.m.?"

"Of course, but they're usually emergencies."

"So you naturally assume Mr. Kaplan's call was also an emergency."

"Not necessarily, but..."

"But what?"

Cooksen's thin lips tightened. "I don't have to explain my reasoning to you, Ms. McCone."

"Nor mine to you."

"As a citizen, you have a duty—"

"Don't give me any of that duty-as-a-citizen crap! What you're asking is I knuckle under to a bully public official!" I glanced at Jamie and said, "I'm out of here."

Jamie caught up with me in the reception area. "Kind of harsh with Cooksen, weren't you?"

"Not harsh enough. He's the kind of cop who enjoys bullying—witness, suspect, jaywalker, you name it. Watch him, because one of these days he's going to take it too far. And the department will suffer for it."

Jamie frowned. "He's not such a bad guy..."

But the rest of what he said didn't compute for me. Suddenly I was picturing the wound on Zack's shoulder. And now I thought I knew where I'd seen one like it before.

I hurried to the stairwell and out of the building to my car.

THURSDAY, AUGUST 11

12:43 a.m.

I pulled to the curb in front of the Breakers about two minutes before Hy arrived in his car. I'd called him after leaving the morgue, told him what had happened to Zack Kaplan, and asked him to meet me here with my new digital camera.

He parked and got out, came up to me where I was leaning against Zack's Jeep. "I assume you want to take photographs of that wall gallery."

"Right. Yesterday I asked Cap'n Bobby for a spare key to the place so we don't have to enter by the crazy hole in the foundation."

"Who in hell created it, anyway?"

"The hole? I would guess Zack Kaplan. As to why—who knows?"

As I led him through the house, Hy was fascinated. "It's an interesting place. What did Chelle intend to do with it?"

"She told Cap'n Bobby she was going to renovate it and sell it to a company that manages facilities for disabled veterans."

"He's the one who still owns it?"

"Yeah. He claims he'll put off the closing until she returns—but who knows when or if that'll be."

Hy heard the forlorn tone in my voice and hugged me around the shoulders.

We went upstairs. Chelle's quarters were as I'd left them. I turned on the lights, then removed the screen from the montage wall. Hy stood staring at the ugly array of clippings and photos, his mouth twisted in distaste.

The montage blurred for me in the poor light. The killers' photos melded into one horrible image of evil. My brow grew damp and I felt the first symptoms of vertigo. Then the bad feelings ebbed, and my focus became sharp as I scanned the old clippings.

After a while I shook my head. "I thought I saw something more here, but now it doesn't stand out."

"Maybe you didn't see it on that wall but somewhere else."

"Maybe, but I'm pretty sure it was here..."

"These monsters all seem familiar—the Manson family, Dan White, Scott Peterson. No gang killers, though."

"Dammit, all the details in these newspaper photos look blurry in this light. I was afraid of that."

"Hence the camera."

"Right. I'll take close-up shots of everything here. The details should be clear in the pics."

"Let's hope so." Hy continued staring at the wall. "Who the devil constructed this thing?"

"I wish I knew. I've canvassed as much of the neighborhood as I can, put operatives on it too. Our researchers haven't come up with a connection either."

"Then you and I had better come up with one."

I photographed the wall and surrounding areas. Hy nosed around and said, just as I finished, "Hey, look at this."

He was standing at the far end of the wall, pointing up toward the ceiling.

"The paper's curling there, as if somebody ripped it."

"Can you see behind what's torn?"

He searched in his pockets, took out a penknife, and probed. "Strange. It looks like there're more items behind these. Maybe a whole other collage." He probed some more. "Yeah, that's what I think it is."

"If so, it should be preserved as is."

"Preserve it on film. Then I'll pull this top layer down."

I took a picture of the curling paper, the flash once more reflecting brightly off the sinister images. Then Hy began delicately peeling off the surface material. I crowded against him, peering up to see what he'd revealed.

Scenic pictures of the sea and sand and wildflowers. The Breakers in its heyday, formally attired ladies and gentlemen flocking to its doors. Familiar faces I'd seen in a social history of the city: Haases and Lilienthals and Crockers, the women all impeccably coiffed and gowned. No killers or other criminals there, just a historical version of the local social register. An early photo of the Cliff House, wreathed in fog.

I said, "So somebody saw this wall and decided to create one with a different motif."

"Radically different."

"I need to talk with Patrick about that ledger of former tenants of Cap'n Bobby's, but I'll get to that in the morning."

8:11 a.m.

We'd been so tired when we got home that we went straight to bed. I was awake at seven, though, with speculations about the investigation crowding my thoughts. Hy was still deeply asleep, the house chilly and the cats snuggled warmly against me. I lay there for a time sorting through what I knew and didn't know so far.

Two possibilities, that either Damon Delahanty or Tyler Pincus was involved in Chelle's disappearance, were now definitely out. I'd checked my voice mail on the drive home. Will had called around eleven. Damon Delahanty, he'd found out, had been incarcerated for the past three weeks in a Clark County, Nevada, jail for armed robbery, bail having been denied. And Tyler Pincus, the magician, had been traveling throughout the Bay Area, trying to salvage his sagging career. Will had been thorough, confirming each man's present whereabouts with the appropriate people.

"Frustrating" was the word for the rest of what I knew. Plenty of questions but no clear-cut answers.

Zack Kaplan had been murdered four days ago, the same night he disappeared from the Breakers. Why? Something to do with the "right to disappear" note? Or for some other reason?

The person who had decorated the wall had nothing to do with this crisis. Or had everything to do with it.

The person who had called me claiming to be Chelle was a fake. Yes, but who was she, and how had she known enough about me and my investigation to attempt extortion?

Chelle had written the note about the right to disappear. Or had she? But if not, who had, and why?

Enough pointless speculating. Time to do something constructive, such as examine the photos that I'd taken at the Breakers.

My camera was on the nightstand. I scanned the digital images, focused on individual areas of the wall montage. The clippings on the Scott Peterson case were the most recent, clustering in the upper right-hand corner and overlapping coverage on the Manson murders. Below them was a one-column piece on Jim Jones's Peoples Temple dated a year before the tragedy in Guyana. Next to it was one of the Zodiac's cryptograms, and above it a photo of the Zebra killers. The Milk/Moscone coverage was there, as was that of the 101 California shooting. But something...

I shook Hy's shoulder. "Ripinsky, wake up. Look at this."

"Huh? What?" He rose on one elbow and rubbed his eyes before staring at me as if I were an alien who had sneaked into his bed.

"These pictures I took of the wall. Something's missing."

"You sure do know how to wake a guy up." He sighed and flopped back against the padded headboard. "What's missing?"

"Some of the clippings."

He took the camera from my hand and examined the image.

"I could swear there was another clipping about the Manson Family," I said. And there were two about Scott Peterson, now there's only one. Check out this article on Felix Mitchell, drug dealer. See this line in the dust?"

My finger traced it and he nodded.

"And there's considerable difference in shading above it where the removed clippings were pinned." I closed my eyes and pictured the wall as I'd first seen it. "There was one on a case I'd never heard of before, illustrated with a drawing. It's not here either."

"You remember what the drawing looked like?"

"Sort of. I think it may have resembled the signature carving on Zack Kaplan's shoulder, but I'm not quite sure." I threw the covers back. "I'd better get moving."

"Where to?"

"Cap'n Bobby's. I have some questions for him."

"Want me to come along?"

"Not necessary. You need to check in at the agency. Somebody's got to run this business of ours."

10:10 a.m.

When I arrived at Cap'n Bobby's, he was seated in his wheelchair going over a pile of receipts with his waitress.

Li said, "I think this supplier is padding his invoices."

"Match the next couple of bills with the orders and call him on it."

"The dishwasher—it's wheezing again."

"Baby it along—we can't afford a new one."

"Right." Li went to the back room and Bobby waved me over.

I sat down at the table beside him. "Did you hear about what happened to Zack Kaplan?"

"Was on the morning news. Too damn bad—he was a nice guy."

"Do you have any idea who might have wanted to kill him?"

"No. Like I said, he was a nice guy; hard to imagine him making any serious enemies. He didn't have much money and no credit cards—when I asked him to pick up something I needed, he'd borrow mine. He studied all the time, was determined to finally get his degree, so he didn't socialize much." He paused. "Must've accidentally crossed paths with some psycho. You know, a random thing—wrong place at the wrong time."

"Maybe," I said. I took out a pad of paper and sketched the wound I'd seen on Zack's shoulder. "Does this symbol look familiar to you?"

He studied it, then shook his head. "Can't say as it does."

"You're sure?"

"Positive. What's it supposed to be?"

"I don't know. Yet."

"Is it important?"

"Whoever killed Zack carved it into his shoulder."

"Jesus. Guy must be some kind of monster."

"That's just what I've been thinking."

11:15 a.m.

At the agency I checked with Ted about Cap'n Bobby's ledgers. His Botany 500 attire was subdued today—

except for a pink-and-orange tie. I'd seen this before when he was about to transition from one fashion statement to another: elements of the current style would disappear, and one day there he'd be in all-new regalia. I hoped this time it would be less like Mannix's TV attire.

"Nothing yet from Patrick on those ledgers," he said, "but I'm expecting results soon. The problem is, business is booming and everybody's overloaded."

"That's not a problem, it's a blessing."

I went down the hallway to my office. The air in there was stuffy, slightly smoky; there had been a big grass fire in Marin last night, according to the morning news, ravaging acres of land and destroying several homes. A typical late-August and autumn hazard here in northern California. The haze over the Bay was so thick I couldn't see the top of Mount Tam. I fiddled with the airflow control, then sat down at my desk and started going through a new stack of paperwork that had appeared in my in-box. Mercifully, I was interrupted by Mick, who had just come into the agency.

"Anything you need me for?" he asked.

"Yes. Take a look at this symbol." I showed him the sketch I'd drawn of the mark carved into Zack Kaplan's shoulder.

Mick leaned over my shoulder. "It looks like a single eye that's been pierced with an arrow. Wait a minute." He took out his iPhone and did a rapid Internet search. "Yeah, I thought so."

"What?"

"It's a version of the evil eye. You know, a curse believed to be cast by a malevolent glare, usually directed at a person when they are unaware. Many cultures believe that receiving the evil eye will cause misfortune or injury."

"Uh-huh. But that doesn't explain what this one actually means."

Mick read off his screen. "Here's more: in ancient Egypt, it was also considered to be a symbol of protection, royal power, and good health." He added wryly, "In this country it could be a symbol for the one percent."

"So this superstition is mainly Egyptian?"

"No, it's worldwide, in its various forms. I can give you details—"

"I don't think I need to go into it so deeply. What I need is a lead to a disturbed person who believes in this stuff. Believes it enough to kill and then carve the symbol into his victims' bodies."

"Victims? Why plural?"

I shrugged. "Just a feeling I have. How about you check into it? If I'm right I can talk with their families and friends. Somebody's got to know something."

"And what does this have to do with Chelle?"

"I think the article that was removed from the killers' wall was about crimes involving an evil eye symbol. Chelle might've read it and connected the symbol with someone she knew. Someone she had reason to fear. That would explain why she fled."

"Not completely. Why wouldn't she have come to you?"

I thought back to where I'd been at the time of her disappearance.

"Because I wasn't available. Hy and I were up at his ranch, getting it ready for sale to the neighbors. We don't have phone service there any more, and I'm sure Chelle didn't have the neighbors' number."

"Well, she could've called you on your cell—or Hy's."

"You're such a child of the tech revolution. She may have tried to, but such devices—unless they're using a local provider—don't work in isolated mountain areas."

"Then why didn't she just go to the police?"

"I've wondered that myself. A young person's distrust of them? There've been a couple of incidents of cops sexually molesting young women in the past year, brutalizing people who shouldn't even have been in custody. A lot of bad publicity. Or more likely she didn't have time, or wasn't sure until it was too late and she gave in to blind fear."

"But if whoever it was she was afraid of caught her at the Curley house, then—"

"Don't say it."

I still refused to consider that Chelle was dead and her body not yet found.

The expression on Mick's face told me he understood why I'd stopped him from voicing the possibility.

1:05 p.m.

I'd just come back from a solitary lunch at Angie's when Ted stepped into my office and said, "Got a preliminary list of names and current whereabouts of former Breakers tenants from the ledgers. There're more to come. So far, most of the names don't appear on the databases we use. A lot of people who lived in that building seem to have been nomads." He handed me a piece of legal paper.

"Thanks. I'll take it from here."

The list contained ten names—not many for the timeline. Three were still in San Francisco, one in Walnut Creek. I started with the SF residents.

Gilda LaPaz: "I never knew anything about a strange wall. But then, my modeling career took me away fairly often...No, I don't recollect anything about a tenant upstairs...I was busy working."

Arthur Zizek: "There was a guy living up there. Studious looking, thick horn-rimmed glasses, always toting an armload of books. He was cordial enough, but he didn't socialize. That's all I remember."

Bruno Storch's voice mail told me he'd call me back if I'd leave a message. I did, explaining what I was looking for.

Sherman Kahn answered his phone in Walnut Creek, but he didn't have anything to tell me either. "Sorry, but I don't remember. That's what shock therapy does to you."

I widened my search.

Don Golden, Reno, Nevada: "I don't remember anybody living up there."

Christopher Lubowski, Ojai: no answer.

Jim Feliz, San Luis Obispo: "How'd you get this number? Don't ever call it again!"

Kimberly Woods, Pensacola, Florida: "There was somebody in that apartment, but he was quiet as a mouse. And 'mouse' is the right term—that building was ridden with them."

No answer at Tina Steinmiller's number in Bakersfield.

The same at Douglas Kemp's in San Diego.

I'd just broken the connection when the phone vibrated with an incoming call. No name, but the number was familiar. A deep male voice said, "Is this Sharon McCone?"

"Yes. And you are?"

"Bruno Storch. You left a message."

"Yes. I was calling about a building in San Francisco, the Breakers, where you lived—"

"Ten, eleven years ago."

"Right. Was your apartment on the middle floor?"

"That's correct."

"In it, there's a wall decorated with a collage of criminal—"

"Is it still there?"

"Yes. Do you remember who made it?"

A long pause. Then he said, "I did."

Ah! I'd finally lucked out. "Can you tell me the reason?"

"Why do you want to know?"

"It pertains to an investigation I'm conducting."

Another pause. "Well, it's a long story, Ms. McCone, and I'd rather not discuss it over my office phone. Can we meet somewhere later today?"

"In public, yes."

"Where are you located?"

"New Montgomery Street."

"I work at Embarcadero Center. How about I meet you at Lucinda's after I get off, if you're free."

"What time do you get off?"

"Four thirty. But I can leave early. How about three thirty? I'll buy you a drink."

"That's not necessary. Dutch treat."

"How will I recognize you?"

I described the black corduroy vest I had on.

"Okay. I'll be there by three thirty. See you then."

3:35 p.m.

Lucinda's was only a few blocks away on the Embarcadero. Once a shack serving fried seafood, it was now more upscale but still specialized in fried seafood. The grease from the fryers didn't smell nearly as bad as the smoke haze from Marin that hung over the outside deck, so I took an inside booth near the windows.

Wildfires. I shuddered. There's nothing in nature that I respect and fear like fire raging out of control.

I watched the entrance and the people who entered. At 3:35 a man came in alone. He was big, in his fifties, with an oversize belly protruding the front of his blue dress shirt. His eyes looked tiny in the flesh that pooched out around them, but they were kind. He looked around, spotted me, and waved.

"Mr. Storch?" I said as he came up to the booth.

"Yes. Ms. McCone?" I nodded, and he extended his hand; it was like a paw, its back hairy.

"Thank you for meeting me on such short notice."

"Likewise."

Storch eased his bulk into the booth. A waiter appeared and he ordered a bourbon on the rocks. I already had my glass of white wine.

"Now, Mr. Storch," I said, "about the montage on the wall of your former apartment at the Breakers."

"Yes. You wanted to know why I put it there."

"A long story, you said on the phone."

He sighed. "I was going through a bad time. My wife had died—cancer—and I was between jobs and not in any shape to go out looking for work. Didn't need to then because I had enough money to live on from her insurance. I read a lot. Brought home big stacks of books from the library every week. That's when I got interested in true crime. Soon I was researching cases on microfilm, having the librarians make copies of the articles. And cutting clippings from the newspapers." He shook his head, sighed again. "It got to be an obsession. That's the kind of personality I have."

"And that's where the idea for the wall came from?"

"Yes. It already had a collage of pretty San Francisco pictures that a former tenant had put up a long time before and that I didn't much like. The city had begun wearing on me; I'd looked beneath its surface and realized it wasn't as pretty—in any sense—as it pretended to be. So after I started on this true-crime kick I thought, *Why not a killers' wall? Let it show how things really are.* And there you have it."

His bourbon on the rocks arrived, and he took a long pull of the drink. When he set the glass down, I asked, "Were you familiar with all the cases you posted there?"

"Some. Others I just posted because I had a space to fill."

"The reason I ask, there were cases I couldn't place, and I've been investigating in the city for many years."

"Which cases?"

"One in particular with illustrations of a symbol that resembles an eye with an arrow through it."

"Oh, sure. I know that one, all right. A funny kind of evil eye, different from any of the other signatures—criminals' individual marks—I've studied."

Now maybe I was getting somewhere. "You've made a study of such things?"

"Yes. The evil eye for good reason." He fumbled with his briefcase, looking faintly embarrassed, and produced an oversize paperback book. He pushed it across the table at me. The title was *Where Are They Now?*

"It's not much," Storch said. "Unsolved cases from the Central Coast area, where I lived in the early two thousands. I published the book myself a few years ago because no mainstream publisher would bother with it. Not enough scope, they said. Small towns, low concept. But the victims' families appreciated them. Somebody's got to acknowledge the victims and their suffering. *Where Are They Now?* incorporates a chapter on the Carver."

The Carver?

I picked the book up. A cover blurb, from a newspaper I'd never heard of, said, "Tense...riveting...one of a kind." Another praised "the clarity of the writing" and professed to have "loved pages fifty to sixty."

Storch said, "Those quotes aren't exactly raves from the *New York Times*, but they made a few people crack the covers." He grinned self-consciously. "I ought to appreciate them; I wrote both."

"You struck the right tone."

"Well, the crimes didn't get much play in the media up here—four killings occurred in and around San Luis Obispo. The victims were all men, stabbed viciously. The killer left his signature carved on the bodies."

"Where on the bodies?"

"Their shoulders."

"Carved after the victims were dead?"

"Yes."

"Was the killer ever identified?"

"No."

"Suspects?"

"None."

"What about a motive for the crimes?"

"None that the police could figure. Had to be some sort of homicidal rage. The Carver's victims seem to have been picked at random. That's my theory, anyway."

"When was the last of the murders?"

"Seven years ago, as far as anybody knows." Storch swallowed more bourbon. "Why are you interested in that symbol, Ms. McCone? Do you have reason to think the Carver's active again, by any chance?"

Yes, but I wasn't about to reveal that to him. I dodged his question by asking, "May I have this book?"

"Sure, it's all yours. I've got a garage full."

"Thanks. Did you write it while you lived at the Breakers?"

"No, after I moved to my apartment in the Inner Sunset, on Ninth Avenue."

"Why did you leave the Breakers?"

"I've got arthritis, and the damp got into my joints. Besides, a new element had moved in out there, and I didn't much like it."

"What sort of element?"

"Violent scumbags—you know the type."

Like the ones who had tried to pick me up at the seawall.

"Have you ever been back to the Breakers?"

"Nope. No reason to. I didn't have much to do with the other tenants while I was there, and like I told you, that collage was part of my obsessive-compulsive period. I sure didn't want to revisit that."

Well, who would?

5:10 p.m.

The first thing I did when I returned to the agency was to run a search to find out if there was any new information on the Carver murders. The office was quiet, most of the staff gone for the day. A light shone under the door of the cubicle shared by Mick and Derek, and I heard the tapping of keys. Had to be Mick, still hard at work, and I didn't want to bother him with a relatively simple task. Derek was still tending to family matters in southern California.

The coverage on the Carver case was sketchy, as Storch had said. The victims had been stabbed with some kind of long-bladed knife, then marked with the crude symbol—not described in the press as the evil eye but as "an eye pierced by an arrow." After four slayings in the San Luis Obispo area and one loosely attributed to him in Santa Maria, he dropped off the media's radar. No new information had surfaced in the past seven years.

I picked up the book Bruno Storch had given me, took it to my armchair, and read the chapter about the Carver and his crimes.

The Carver must have acted alone. The police found no evidence at the crime scenes to suggest a second killer, and no one came forward to identify him in exchange for immunity from prosecution. Either he had avoided incarceration on other charges or he wasn't a talker; there were no jailhouse rumors or other talk about him. One can imagine a quiet individual with no outstanding physical features, a Walter Mitty without a nagging mother to quiz him about his every move.

Did he set out to kill or was he motivated by impulse? Why were his victims all men? Four of the murders happened in the San Luis area, indicating a strong connection there. The weapon, never recovered, was the same in all cases, according to police lab reports.

In seven months, this unknown man murdered at least four people, butchering them with a knife and carving his signature symbol on their bodies.

What is this symbol's secret meaning? What cult claims it as its own?

How many more Carvers are out there awaiting their chance to wreak mayhem?

Conspiracy theory mixed with a true-crime approach, I thought, shaking my head. And not very well written.

My approach to investigation has always been to look for the obvious first. Too many of us search for the complicated solution, only to find out that the motive for and commission of a given crime are actually quite simple.

I skimmed through the rest of the book. Psychological profiles of serial killers; details of various killings; investigative leads/lines; principal investigators; false/unproven leads; suspects; outcomes of suspect interviews; reports; conclusions.

Bruno Storch had done his homework, but there was nothing but weak, unsubstantiated speculation as to what the Carver's motive might have been. Even when he slipped into passages that attempted to describe what kind of man the killer was, they contained very little insight.

Seven years since the last known Carver killing was a long time. The authorities would have back-burnered the case when no new leads appeared. But now one had, Zack Kaplan's murder, and the authorities seemed not to be following up on it.

Well, it was a cold case. And police departments are overburdened; the connection to the Carver likely hadn't been made yet. Plus there was the fact that Zack hadn't been anybody important. The body of an underemployed man tossed in a vacant lot wasn't a priority. Never mind the cryptic symbol carved into his shoulder, which somebody should have remembered having seen before. Never mind that my agency—well known to the police—had reported him as a missing person.

If Zack Kaplan's killer was the Carver, what was the connection between them? Had Kaplan somehow figured out who he was and foolishly gone to confront him? Was that why the clipping had been removed from the wall montage? And then there were the seven years of inactivity; what had the Carver been doing all that time? Common sense said the most likely explanation was that he'd been in prison or some kind of mental health facility.

I wondered if anyone connected with Chelle had ties in the San Luis Obispo area, and paged through Will Camphouse's reports. No mention of the college town or other Central Coast communities, but I'd interrupt Mick after all and ask him to dig deeper on a priority basis. For a moment I debated calling Jamie Strogan, but decided against it. I had no solid evidence of a connection between the Carver killings and Chelle's disappearance. It was too soon to take unfounded suspicions to the authorities.

5:55 p.m.

There was nothing more to occupy me at the office. And Hy had a business dinner, so I was in no hurry to go home. For want of anything better to do, I decided to return to the Breakers, check through Zack's effects again on the off chance I'd missed something linking him to the missing clipping.

The old building creaked and groaned in a strong offshore wind. Although, thanks to daylight saving time, it was bright and sunny outside, the interior was filled with gloom. The familiar pervasive odor of mold and decay filled the air. I tried the light switch in the foyer, but nothing happened; PG&E hadn't received my request that the service be put in the agency's name before terminating it. That was the utility's modus operandi: slow on customer service but fast with the off switch. I turned on my flashlight as I went down the narrow hall to Zack's room.

A sweep with the flashlight showed nothing had changed there. Zack had been a loner, with no relatives to collect his belongings; the police hadn't yet investigated here, and I doubted they would. I set the flashlight on top of a battered bureau and began going through it.

Socks, most of them with holes in the toes. Jockey shorts, in similar disrepair. T-shirts, a summer-weight robe, and sweats. Jeans. An empty bottom drawer. A row of ragged athletic shoes lined up against the wall next to the bureau, outerwear hung on pegs above them. Some bricks and boards were stacked next to the bed—a combination bookcase and nightstand. The books were mainly textbooks or from the library, although there were some trade paperbacks that looked as if he'd picked them up at a thrift shop. The subjects were eclectic: astronomy, physics, philosophy; sudoku and crossword puzzles; mystery novels and police procedurals that bolstered my impression he might have considered himself an amateur detective; Westerns and science fiction. A reading light, an iPod and earphones, a Japanese bowl containing loose change, and a pair of binoculars sat on the top shelf.

I picked up the binoculars and focused them through the single window. Nothing but a solid brick wall a couple of lots away. I trained them down at a weedy and junk-filled lot; a couple of small kids were rooting around in a pile of garbage bags. One of them came up with something valuable—to him—and ran off with it; the other followed, screeching, "Mine! Mine!"

After a quick inventory of the bathroom—no drugs, prescription or otherwise, in the medicine chest, and mainly dirty towels and sheets stuffed into a hamper— I gave up my search. Zack had led a sad, depressing life, and its evidence made me grateful for all I had in mine.

6:45 p.m.

When I emerged from the building I found Ollie Morse sitting on the front steps. He looked depressed and was trying to uproot a weed from where it had taken hold in the grout between the bricks.

"Hey, Ollie," I said, and sat down beside him.

He glanced at me, his eyes blank for a moment. "Sharon, right?"

"Right. Okay if I sit here with you?"

"Sure. I'm just waiting for Al so we can go get supper. We've got a small shop on Innes down near the shipyards where we keep tools and stuff for our construction jobs. He couldn't find his wire strippers, thought he might've left them at the shop. Or maybe here, so he sent me over to check, but I couldn't find them."

"Did you hear the news about Zack Kaplan?" I asked.

"Who? Oh, yeah. Bummer."

"When did you see him last?"

He shrugged. "Don't remember."

"You've been on the floor where Chelle was staying. Remember the wall with all the clippings on it?"

"Yeah. So?"

His replies weren't combative or evasive; his blank stare and lack of inflection were the same as before.

"When was the last time you were up there?"

"I dunno. Al says—"

He didn't get to tell me what Al said, because just then a shabby white pickup truck rattled to a stop behind Ollie's, and Al stepped out.

"Hey, Sharon," he said as he approached. He perched on the step below us. "Any news about Chelle?"

"Nothing so far. I'm working on it."

"That why you're here?"

"Yes. Checking Zack's apartment."

"Zack. Hell of a thing, what happened to him. You don't think him getting killed has anything to do with Chelle?"

I hedged on that. "I don't know, it might."

"Sure hope not. What were you and Ol talking about?"

"This old wreck of a building and the wall on the floor where Chelle was staying."

"Depressing subject." He turned to Ollie. "Look," he said, "why don't you go home, clean up, change your shirt, and then meet me at the Inferno?"

"Right." Ollie stood, suddenly eager to get going.

As he hurried along the sidewalk to his pickup, Al said to me, "We've got apartments in the same building on Forty-Seventh Avenue. He needs somebody to watch over him. PTSD, you know?"

I nodded, watching Ollie drive off. "Must be kind of hard on you."

"It's what a buddy does. Besides, Ol's pretty self-sufficient if nothing sets him off."

"What sets him off?"

"The usual PTSD stuff—sudden loud noises, flash-backs."

"How does he react?"

"Freezes up, mostly. Freaks out now and then—I give him tranquilizers when that happens."

"But he's able to work regularly?"

"More or less. Disability pays most of the bills. They're enough for him to get by, but they should be higher. Ol fought and almost died for this country, and what does it give him? Or me or any of us? Only enough to get by!"

I agreed with him.

Al stood. "I gotta go, Ms. McCone. Ol'll be waiting."

I remained seated on the steps for a while after he'd gone. I knew something about PTSD, because I'd read up on it and talked to a couple of physicians, hoping it might have some connection to what was wrong with my half brother Darcy, and wondering if it had contributed to my brother Joey's overdose. No connection had appeared, so I'd finally given up.

Primarily, PTSD involves a trigger—a traumatic event that causes the person who experienced it to relive the experience or avoid situations that are re-minders of it. The disease may appear from one month after the event to an indefinite number of years later. If exposed to such memories, the in-dividual can have many responses: physical pain, flashbacks, or nightmares; depression or anxiety; paranoia; fear of objects connected with the trauma. Irritability, lack of concentration, and sleeplessness are also symptoms. To say nothing of risky behavior

("I can climb the Golden Gate Bridge"); avoidance ("I don't need nobody"); repression ("I can't remember"); emotional numbing ("Can't feel a thing for that asshole"); and hyperarousal ("I'm so nervous I can't sit still").

Okay, how had Ollie scored on my personal—albeit inexpert—PTSD test?

Traumatic event: Combat in Afghanistan. Reliving the experience in flashback.

Physical pain: Ollie didn't show evidence of it, but you couldn't always observe that.

Sleeplessness: Probably.

Nightmares: Again, probably.

Depression: Not that I could tell, but who can see into another person's emotional state?

Irritability: Ollie was an even-tempered man, as far as I knew.

Lack of concentration: Yes.

Risky behavior: Maybe crossing against the red light when traffic was coming, but otherwise he didn't seem like a daredevil.

Avoidance: Ollie was gregarious, and friendly enough except when he was drinking; then women gave him "the red ass."

Emotional numbing: Not the man who was so concerned for Chelle.

Hyperarousal: Hardly.

Ollie's score on my amateur PTSD test was ambiguous. As with any disease or psychological syndrome, not everyone fit all the symptoms. And not everyone who fit some of them had the malady. Lord knows we all have our quirks. I should know—I've developed a lion's share of them.

7:41 p.m.

Mick called as I was driving to Danny's Inferno. He'd been unable to find any direct or indirect connection to the San Luis area for Chelle or any of the other principals in the case, now or from seven years ago. He'd keep digging.

"A couple of other things," he said then. "Some guy named Rosie—a *man*, no less—phoned to say that his truck was found wrecked in the Santa Cruz Mountains. It's a total loss, but he's talked his insurance agent into full replacement cost, so he's happy."

"He have any idea how the truck got there?"

"It had been hot-wired, so the cops figured it was stolen. Then they got a report that it had been used in a convenience store robbery in San Jose—two guys, both black."

That seemed to end any possible connection between the delivery truck and Zack's murder. He'd used the truck to make his rounds for Rosie, then gone to lunch or whatever, and come out to find the truck gone. But why hadn't he notified the police or Rosie? Well, there was probably some simple explanation. Maybe he'd parked it in a tow-away zone, mistakenly figured it had been towed, and hadn't told Rosie because he was trying to scrape together enough money to pay the city ransom. And been murdered before he could.

Mick went on, "Also, that PI Eric Lopez you use in Sacramento told me he's located the girl who phoned you pretending to be Chelle. Her name's Anna Teel. She's a waitress at the Capitol City Café, and a friend of hers asked her to make the call to you."

"And the friend is?"

"Woman named Li Huang. Another waitress, works for—"

"I know who she works for. Cap'n Bobby."

7:59 p.m.

I slammed into Cap'n Bobby's and went straight to the end of the bar where Li Huang sat sucking on a plastic straw and staring at a sitcom on TV. There was nobody else in the place, fortunately, except for O'Hair. When Huang saw the expression on my face, her facial muscles tightened and she turned on her stool as if to leave.

I was too quick for her. I grabbed her by the faux fur collar of her black spandex vest and spun her around. Pulled her up until her face was nearly level with mine, taking a perverse pleasure in the fear that clouded her eyes.

"Hey, ladies!" O'Hair started to roll toward us.

I stopped him by holding up my free hand like a traffic cop. "This is between Ms. Huang and me, Bobby."

She took the distraction as an opportunity to escape. I yanked her back.

"You," I said, "are a contemptible human being!"

"I didn't do anything!"

"You promised your friend Anna Teel two hundred dollars if she called me pretending to be Chelle Curley and tried to get me to give her five thousand dollars. That's extortion."

Cap'n Bobby was shocked. "Why, Li? Why'd you do a crazy thing like that?"

She tried to squirm out of her jacket, but I twisted it by the hood and held her close.

"Why?" I repeated.

"It was just... opportunity."

"Explain that."

"Chelle is missing, and I heard you telling Bobby how close the two of you are, and I thought..."

"Thought you could make a quick, easy score."

"I needed the money. Bills, and my rent's overdue..."

"I ought to have you arrested and prosecuted for attempted extortion. You and your friend both. Maybe I will," I added, though I knew I wouldn't. The attempt had failed and I had enough things to take up my time without filing a police report that would require yet another court appearance. "I'll have to think about it."

Cap'n Bobby, his face crimson, pointed his chair toward the back of the restaurant. "See me in my office, Li," he said.

I let go of her, and she grasped the bar stool she'd been sitting on, hanging her head so her hair covered her face. "Now look what you did to me; I'm going to lose my job!"

No sense of responsibility there. And no sense either. Scammers are all around us—and they're all stupid.

8:39 p.m.

Danny's Inferno was crowded, but I spotted Pamela Redfin serving customers in a booth at the rear. She waved when she saw me pushing through the tightly packed bodies.

"So what brings you here tonight?" she asked when she finished serving. "News about Chelle?"

"No. More questions for you and your father."

She glanced around at the crowd. "Danny and I will have to visit with you in shifts," she said. "Most nights are busy, but not like this. We had to bring in a part-time helper. Are you drinking white wine?"

She went to get it for me. A couple left another booth while she was gone, and I claimed it quickly before anyone else did. When Pamela returned, she said as she set the glass down, "So what do you want to know?"

"I'll try to be brief. I may have already asked you this, but when was the last time you saw Zack Kaplan?"

"Hmmm. Last weekend, maybe." She sighed. "I saw on the news about his murder. Awful."

"Do you know of any reason why someone would want to kill him?"

"No. Zack got along with everybody, at least in here."

"Has anyone been around asking about him recently?"

"No one I know of besides you. You don't think one of our customers could have sliced him up that way—?"

"No, I'm just trying to cover all the possibilities."

"Well..." People at a nearby table began clamoring for refills. "I better get hopping. I'll send Danny over first chance he gets."

I sipped wine while I waited for her father and listened idly to the chattering voices around me.

"...I can't imagine what goes on in that pinhead of hers, but..."

"...and the diamond in the engagement ring was as tiny as his dick..."

"...I'm not saying sexual harassment is right, but that was just the way things were in the eighties..."

Danny Redfin joined me. He was decked out in his usual devil's attire, plus a peaked cap whose shadow gave his eyebrows an appropriate Satanic cast. He resembled Satan too: his eyes were red and fiery with both anger and grief. "So Pammy says you've got more questions. About Zack Kaplan, I suppose. God, I hope they catch the crazy son of a bitch who butchered him."

"Whoever it is won't get away with it."

"Better not." He exhaled loudly and sat down. "Zack was a little flaky, but I liked him. Now and then him and me, and Al and Ollie, spent some free time together away from here."

"Doing what?"

"Bowling, watching sports on TV, hanging out. Guy stuff."

"When was the last time you saw him?"

"I think about a week ago. I could ask the others. In my business I see so many people that the times and days when they come in kind of blend together."

"Do you know of anybody who held a grudge against him?"

"Zack? Hell no!"

"Did he ever talk about the Breakers?"

"Not much. Strange damn place, I don't understand why he chose to live there."

"Inertia, he told me. Staying was easier than moving."

"Zack could be kind of an inert guy."

"Did he ever mention a wall montage there?"

"Oh, yeah. All the serial killers. Did you know Chelle was actually living in that unit?"

"Yes."

"Another thing I don't understand. There's a lot I don't understand, I guess."

"Do you know anybody who lived in the San Luis Obispo area seven years ago?"

"San Luis? No. Why?"

I didn't have to give him an answer because just then Pamela called him back to the bar. That was all right with me. All the noise in there was giving me a headache, and I had no more questions to ask him anyway.

10:21 p.m.

Hy drove into the garage as I was watching a particularly bad TV movie without paying much attention to it. When he entered the house, he sat down next to me on the sofa, moving my legs onto his lap. "What's that?" he asked, motioning at the TV.

"It's called *Help Me! Help Me!* And it needs all the help it can get." I thumbed the remote off. "How was your dinner?"

"Looks like we've gotten a new client. Silicon Valley start-up. Small account, but they're going places. I'll give you my notes tomorrow. Anything new on Chelle?"

"Nothing. I did meet with someone who used to live at the Breakers—Bruno Storch, an amateur true-crime writer." I held out Storch's *Where Are They Now?*, open to the chapter on the Carver killings. "You know anything about that case?"

He glanced through the chapter. "Nothing more than you've told me and what's in here. San Luis is a long way from here, and seven years a long time."

"I skimmed the book, but it didn't give me much insight. Mainly vague speculation and information that was documented elsewhere. It's as if Storch were fictionalizing a character whose head he can't possibly get into."

"Or maybe trying to disguise the fact that he knows or suspects the Carver's identity. Or *is* him."

"I had the research department run background on Storch; he was where he claims he was during the critical time frames. And as for knowing who the killer is, why would anyone shelter the identity and whereabouts of someone who committed these kinds of atrocities?"

"You and I wouldn't, but that's us. What about Zack Kaplan? Any connection turn up between him and the San Luis area or the Carver?"

"None that Mick has been able to come up with, or that anybody I talked to knows about."

"You think Zack took the clipping from the wall?"

"More likely it was whoever killed him. What Zack was excited about Saturday night was the 'right to disappear' note. It could be he saw who delivered it and instead of waiting for me, chased after the man. I told you he was enthusiastic about detecting."

"And got himself butchered for it."

"Yes."

"You're sure Chelle wrote that note?"

"It must've been her. Her handwriting is pretty distinctive."

"Which brings us back to the critical question: Is she still alive?"

"I refuse to believe she's dead. She *has* to be alive, wherever she is."

"What about her parents and their disappearance in Costa Rica?"

I shook my head. "That's still a mystery. Julia called me when she first arrived down there and then—silence."

"People disappearing like this. I don't like it, McCone."

"Me either," I said. "Not one damn bit."

Sometime in the dark hours...

I woke to an unearthly silence. There were none of the usual urban sounds.

No late buses or automobiles went past. No one talked on the street. Our electric clock had stopped. I slipped out of bed, threw my robe on, and went to one of the front rooms that had a view of the Marina Green; not a light there either. No lights on the Marin Hills and, most surprising, no lights on the Golden Gate Bridge. It was a massive power outage.

As I stared at the bridge, its lights flickered and went out again. They flickered once more, then blossomed, and the span was restored to its normal luminous intensity. Emergency generator at work.

I hurried downstairs and went out onto the front steps. The air was warm, windy, and very smoky. Lingering fumes from the wildfires in Marin, blowing our way. The flames couldn't jump the Bay, but were licking a wide path of destruction along the waterfront over there.

Fire—my biggest fear, and here I was, physically safe but psychically confronting it again.

Hy came up behind me, put his hands on my shoulders. There was no reason to speak; the scene before us said it all. After a while we went into the house. I am in no way religious, but after we went back to bed I said a prayer for those who were losing their homes and livelihoods—maybe even their very lives. I suspected Hy said one too.

FRIDAY, AUGUST 12

The electricity had been restored, but the air was still smoke laden, and there were advisories on TV against going outside if you didn't have to. I scrounged up a packet of face masks from the garage that a contractor who had been removing asbestos had left behind. If we had to go out, we'd use them.

All day I'd be getting phone calls from friends and relatives asking if we were all right. I tried to reach Julia in Costa Rica, but the call went to her voice mail. The Curleys' cell wasn't operative.

I heard from Mick then, letting me know both he and Derek would be working from their respective homes today, and that he'd be e-mailing me background information on the San Luis area victims of the Carver. The e-mail came a few minutes later.

Ronald Brower, 27, had been working as a bartender to save for his tuition at Cal Poly, where he was majoring in psychology. He was a local, living at home with his divorced mother, a nurse.

No siblings and no father in the picture. He had a girlfriend, Dana Stutz, who could contribute little to the investigation.

Kirk D'Angelo, 33, a software salesman for Micro, Ltd. in Seattle, had been staying at the Days Inn. He'd had dinner at one of the food trucks, then gone for a walk on the pier where he, a gregarious type, had talked with several people. He never returned to his motel, and his body washed up near the municipal pier the next day.

Ward Jamison, 29, a married accountant with two small children, had been working late and was walking through his building's parking lot in a hurry. He'd promised his wife he'd arrive on time at home in Grover Beach for the cake-and-champagne celebration of her father's 60th birthday. He'd been killed in the lot where his car was parked.

Christopher Wickens, 37, a photographer for the local newspaper, was the most well known of the victims. He'd roamed San Luis and the nearby towns with his Leica, snapping both hard news and human interest shots. He was genial and cheerful, openly gay and living with a partner, Clive Canfield, in the hills above town. After he'd been missing for three days, a pair of campers found his body near an old winery in the Santa Lucia Mountains.

David Kristof, 19, was another student at Cal Poly, majoring in history. His parents in the LA suburb of Newport Beach had wanted him to attend USC, but in the end his preference for a change of scene had prevailed. On the night of his death he was seen at various bars and clubs with an ever-changing group of friends, but no one remembered where they'd parted company. His body was discovered in a city park at dawn the next day by joggers.

The police reports had noted no commonalities among the victims. They hadn't known each other, hadn't resided near each other, hadn't had mutual friends or—in the case of the students—shared classes. Random killings, was the assumption. There was more in the reports, much more, dealing with the victims' families, living situations, likes and dislikes, amusements, hobbies, and friends. More than I could absorb at this time.

1:03 p.m.

I finally heard from Julia. The cell service from Costa Rica was spotty today, but except for brief fade-outs we could understand each other well enough.

"I've located the Curleys," she said. "They're about to fly to Washington, D.C., and then to SF."

"Have they heard from Chelle?"

"No. That's the downside—she never contacted them or her brother."

"Damn! So what was this disappearing act they

pulled all about? They were concerned with where she was, and then they just vanished—"

"Shar, do you know what they do?"

"You mean for a living? They own a print shop near the Panhandle."

"That's not their primary occupation, not for the past several years."

"Then what is?"

"Government intelligence operations in Central and South America."

"What!"

"It's true. I wormed it out of a guy in the diplomatic service down here. That's why all the trips. That's why their sudden disappearance."

I still had a hard time believing it. "I lived next door to the Curleys for a number of years, took my printing jobs to their shop, entertained them frequently. Now you tell me they're *spies*?"

"Evidently they were recruited twelve years ago by one of the alphabet agencies—the covert kind that only top government officials know exist."

"The *Curleys*? Why them? What on earth made them recruitable?"

"Seems they met in the military, where they were engaged in similar activities. Their friend said they're highly addicted to adventure."

"Who's this guy in the diplomatic service you talked to?"

"His name's Peterson. He was assigned to perform liaison services for them."

"Why'd he out them to you?"

"He didn't out them exactly. Seems they've had enough of undercover work—they're going to D.C. to resign. Chelle still being missing is what did it. They decided her life is worth more to them than adventure."

"Too bad they didn't figure that out years ago."

"I agree. Say, didn't you once have contact with an alphabet agency?"

"Yeah—CENTAC—years ago. If I hadn't stumbled across them in connection with another case, they'd still be playing their dirty tricks deep in the subbasement of D.C. politics." I paused, then asked, "Was Chelle aware of her folks' covert activities?"

"They say no, but I find that hard to believe."

So did I. The Curleys had always been a close-knit family. Jim and Trish wouldn't have been able to keep their government activities a secret from Chelle once she was an adult. She was too smart and inquisitive.

"Anyway," Julia said, "Mrs. Curley said for me to tell you she'll call you from D.C."

"I'll be waiting." Ungraciously, I cut the call short with a terse thanks and goodbye. Sort of a kill-the-messenger moment.

Immediately I tapped out Mick's cell number. "You're not going to believe what Julia just told me, calling from Costa Rica."

"These days I believe anything. What?"

I explained.

"Doesn't surprise me all that much," he said after a pause. "You know that drawer of crap you had me take from the Curleys' kitchen? Well, I finally got to looking through it this afternoon. Nothing interesting except for a beat-up travel wallet; in one of its inside pockets there was a set of orders dated ten years ago on a MATS flight to Brazil."

MATS: Military Air Transport Service. Used to ferry military personnel to hot spots around the world. And spies?

"Find out all you can about their spook activities," I said, and made another ungracious disconnect.

1:52 p.m.

So what was I supposed to do now? Wait around for Trish to call and her and Jim to get back? It could be a long time; from what I knew of government agencies there would be debriefings and more debriefings. And according to Julia, there wasn't anything they could tell me about Chelle's disappearance anyway. My investigation was at a standstill, I was frustrated and restless, but there had to be *something* I could do . . .

My eyes lighted on the reports on the alleged victims of the Carver in the San Luis area. There was something I could do that might bring results, and would also get me out of the smoky San Francisco air. I copied the parts of the reports containing the names and addresses of friends or relatives of the victims. Then I deposited the documents on Mick's desk and left M&R.

5:18 p.m.

The problem with this case, I thought as I navigated the tricky downhill curves of Highway 101 leading into

San Luis Obispo, was that it had started out only about Chelle being missing, but now had lost its focus and seemed centered not on her but on the Carver. If I didn't turn up a lead on the Central Coast...Well, worry about that if and when the time came.

San Luis is a Mission town, founded by Franciscan Junípero Serra. Serra's reasoning—that the native Chumash Indians were friendly and the cool Mediterranean climate pleasant and amply supplied with fresh water and game—was proven out, and over the years the town grew to a population in the mid-forty-thousands, augmented every fall by the influx of students at Cal Poly, one of the west's best polytechnic institutions.

The town was crowded on this mid-August Friday, even though classes hadn't yet started: tourists walked slowly, snapping photographs; beachgoers hustled across the hot streets, sunburned and wrapped in towels; people ate ice cream cones and by-the-slice pizza. There were rollerbladers and skateboarders and bus tours for the elderly, their leaders bellowing through microphones. An overpowering aroma of sea air, popcorn, and frying oil filled the air.

Ted—after several tries—had gotten me a reservation at the Seaside Inn, only a short walk from the Port San Luis Pier. An attractive, comfortable place with Wi-Fi. I set up my laptop and checked in with the agency. Ted had managed to schedule me appointments with two of the victims' relatives for this evening.

7:10 p.m.

Alida Washington, aunt of Christopher Wickens, lived in the foothills on the eastern side of the freeway. She was young to be the aunt of a fortysome-year-old man, clad in tight-fitting shorts and a halter top, with dark crescents under her nails that showed she'd been working in the garden.

"Fall veggies," she said, leading me to a screened porch at the rear of her house. "You've gotta get them in the ground on time. Would you like a beer?"

"Sure."

She went into what must be a kitchen and came back with two frosty Heinekens. "So you're here about Christopher?" she said, sitting down. "Why? It's old news."

"Maybe not as old as it might seem."

"You've found out something about who did this horrible thing to him?"

"Possibly. Tell me about Christopher."

"He was a good man. One of the best. And talented. Have you seen any of his photographs?"

"No, I haven't."

She motioned at the wall across from us. "Those two are his."

Black and white with impressive shadowing. The nearby hills as few had ever seen them, one taken in early morning, the other near dusk.

"He *was* talented," I said. "And, I understand, well liked."

"Very well liked. I don't think he had an enemy in the world. How someone could just...cut him up like that..."

"Can you think of anything he might've done to provoke it?"

Many people would have said an immediate no, but Alida Washington stopped and thought. The no came a moment later. "Random, the sheriff's department said."

"Perhaps he tried to take the wrong person's picture?"

Her eyes widened. "Maybe. He liked to take candid shots. But he always got permission and a signed release."

"Did you tell law enforcement that?"

"Oh, yes. They searched his files and office, but found nothing."

"What happened to Christopher's camera—the one he was using that day?"

"The Leica? The Santa Lucia County Sheriff's Department still has it. They're supposed to return it to me if they ever close out the case." She snorted disdainfully.

"Did Christopher ever use another camera?"

"Just the Leica. I let them take it, but I didn't give them his camera bag. I needed to have something to remember him by."

Camera bag: a repository for all kinds of items. "May I see it?"

"Certainly." She got up and went into the house. I relaxed for a moment, listening to a pair of jays quarreling in the pines at the back of the lot.

Alida came back out. "Here it is." She thrust the bag at me.

It was in bad shape, caked with mud, its shoulder strap torn.

"Where was this found?"

"I myself found it in the wheel well of the trunk of his car after the police returned it to me. They either hadn't noticed it or didn't realize what it was."

"And where was the camera?"

"Downhill from his body, in the Santa Lucia Mountains. He had an assignment to do a photo essay on the area for the local paper. There's a packet of photos of that wilderness area inside. I suppose the bag was in the trunk because he wouldn't want it hanging off him in such rough terrain."

"May I take this with me?" I asked. "I promise to bring it back to you as soon as possible."

"Keep it. I can't be forever clinging to the past. Better yet, give it to Clive. I've been meaning to."

"Clive?"

"Chris's partner."

"I'll be happy to do that," I said.

7:53 p.m.

I opened the bag in my car, found the packet of photos. Redwoods, light filtering down through their high branches; three young deer playing in a meadow; exotic mushrooms and ferns; crystal water rippling over smooth stones; a rustic bridge with something dark lurking under it; an ancient willow tree, splitting apart except where an iron bar held its two main trunks together.

Something dark there too. Figures—males, I thought. The shadows under the footbridge and in the tangle of tree limbs obscured them, but I got the sense of leanness and flexibility from the way they stood. The juxtaposition of light and shadow cast a threatening aura over the otherwise pastoral scenes. The two dark figures seemed to be waiting for something or someone.

Christopher Wickens, who had stumbled into their territory? Christopher, who was soon to become their prey?

The rest of the bag's contents didn't tell me much. Extra lens caps—a necessity for most pros because the caps have a habit of falling off and vanishing forever. Lens-polishing cloths, carefully folded in an inside pocket. Four canisters of unexposed film. Kodak infrared, ISO 400. Good for use in poor visibility or at night. Had there been film in the Leica when it was found? If so, the sheriff's department technicians would have developed it long ago.

In the other pockets: Nail clippers. Comb, retaining few of its teeth. Small baggie of marijuana. Rolling papers and Bic lighter. Magnifying glass and jeweler's loupe for examining prints. Kleenex packet. ATM withdrawal slip for a hundred dollars. Map of Santa Lucia County, with Santa Marta Creek—a village in the Santa Lucia Mountains, judging from the tiny size of the dot—circled in black felt tip.

Santa Marta Creek. I'd go there tomorrow.

8:20 p.m.

According to Mick's detailed information, a cocktail waitress named Dana Stutz had been the girlfriend of bartender Ronald Brower. She worked at Water's Edge, an upscale bar near my motel. She was on duty tonight, and willing to sit down with me during her break. She was tall but fragile looking, with pale skin that seemed nearly translucent. Her black hair was restrained tightly at the nape of her neck.

"I can't imagine why you want to talk to me about Ron after all this time. Unless there's new evidence about his murder...?"

"Potentially there is, but I can't discuss it yet."

"The police said Ron didn't know the crazy person who killed him, that he was in the wrong place at the wrong time."

"That seems likely. Will you tell me about the last time you saw him?"

"We were working different shifts—he was just coming on, I was going home—so we only had time to talk in passing."

"About...?"

"Plans for the weekend, nothing special. Maybe dinner with friends, maybe a movie. I don't know." She shrugged. "It doesn't matter now."

"Were you two living together, if you don't mind my asking?"

"No, we weren't." She wrinkled her nose. "His mother wouldn't allow it."

"Why not?"

"She *needed* him at home, she said."

"I take it you and his mother weren't close."

"That's an understatement. I haven't had anything to do with her since Ron was killed."

"How did he cope with the situation?"

"By walking a tightrope. He couldn't quite break

loose of her, and I was at the point that I'd had it. In fact, I was going to break up with him that weekend. But then...a friend of mine saw it on the news the next noon and called me. I couldn't believe it until I turned on the TV. His body was found in an alley two blocks from here. They had his mother on the broadcast for a few minutes, and she was wailing and screaming, saying something about his awful companions. They cut her off before she could get to me."

"Grief does weird things to people."

"And makes weird people even weirder. She called me up the next day and made all sorts of ridiculous accusations."

"Such as?"

"That I'd cast some sort of spell on Ron. Said that I'd put the 'evil eye' on him."

That startled me. What did Ron Brower's mother know of the evil eye?

"Did she explain what she meant by that?"

"No, she wasn't in any explaining mode."

"Did Ron ever mention an evil eye to you?"

"Never. I don't even know what it is."

9:05 p.m.

Ronald Brower's mother, Mrs. Celia Brower, consented to see me at nine o'clock. On the phone she came across as anything but the "mother from hell" Dana had made her out to be. She was pleasant enough and willing to talk to me tonight, despite the lateness of the hour, and readily provided directions to her home near the Cal Poly campus.

The Brower house was redwood and glass, nestled among pines on a large lot. I rang the bell. The woman who came to the door had short gray hair cut in a chic style and wore an elegant dark-green silk lounging outfit. She shook my hand and ushered me into a large foyer overlooked by two stories of railed galleries. The furnishings of the foyer were minimal—a bench here, an ornamental urn there—but the hardwood floors were partially covered by luminous Oriental carpets in rich shades of red, cobalt blue, orange, and vermillion.

Celia Brower led me to a formal living room. Uncomfortable-looking sofas and chairs were grouped in front of a fireplace, tables with parquet designs protected by glass interspersed between them. The fireplace showed no sign of use. My hostess motioned for me to sit. The sofa felt as it looked—rock hard.

I said, "As I explained on the phone, I have a reason for reopening the investigation of your son's death—"

"Has the maniac who killed Ronald begun slaughtering people again, if he ever stopped?"

"He may have. I can't say for sure."

"Do you know or suspect who he is?"

"Not yet."

"I pray to God you find out. But I don't know how I can help you."

"I know seven years is a long time, but there may be something you can tell me that might be useful. I've already spoken with Dana Stutz—"

"That woman!" Celia Brower's face contorted with anger. "She's to blame for what happened to Ronald!"

"In what way?"

"She talked him into taking that ridiculous bartending job. He told me he needed the money, but I'd have gladly given it to him. No, he said, he wanted to pay for his college on his own. That damned independent streak—he got it from his father. Then the hussy wanted Ronald to move in with her. I told him I needed him here—it was true; I have a weak heart. He was a dutiful son and he stayed. The night he was attacked and murdered, he was walking back to his car from that dreadful bar."

"Dana told me you claimed she put the evil eye on your son. What did you mean by that?"

"The evil eye? How dare she! I said no such thing to her."

"She seemed positive that you had."

"Nonsense. I never did. She's a terrible liar, that woman, among her other faults."

I didn't press the issue. If Mrs. Brower had used the term "evil eye," it could have been in the heat of the moment—the raving of a grieving mother.

I let a few seconds pass and then asked, "What can you tell me about your son? His studies, his interests, his leisure time activities?"

For a moment she looked blank. "Well...he was majoring in psychology. Personally, I didn't think that was right for him."

"Oh? Why?"

"Ronald wasn't a people person. He was all right behind a bar, I suppose, where the rules are clearly defined, but in a social situation he was hopeless."

"Hopeless?"

"He didn't relate. At parties—I give many parties— he would simply sit apart from the group and watch people. If they spoke with him, he was perfectly polite, but he had a reserve that—one of my friends described it as icy."

"Yet he was a good son to you?"

"Very good. Dutiful, as I said."

"What about interests, hobbies?"

"He had none. He was always studying."

"Was he a sports fan?"

"He didn't care for spectator sports. He did play tennis with his father."

"I understand his father was no longer in his life."

"He is no longer in *this* life. He died in an auto accident ten years ago. It was nowhere near as great a loss to me as Ronald's death, I assure you."

Dana had the right take on Mrs. Brower after all, I decided. She *was* something of a "mother from hell."

10:15 p.m.

When I'd called Clive Canfield, Christopher Wickens's partner, earlier, he'd told me to drop around any time I pleased. "I'll be up till all hours," he said. His voice had sounded flat, but he seemed to be glad at the prospect of having company.

His small adobe home was perched on a ridge about a mile from Celia Brower's house. But there was no resemblance between the two dwellings. The Canfield place was warm and welcoming, with none of the stylized perfection of the Browers'. As in Chris's aunt's house, enlarged prints of Christopher's photos covered the walls. Comfortable chairs were placed close to the hearth, and the floor plan was designed to flow into one big room with a sleeping gallery upstairs. Clive Canfield fitted its style: slightly pudgy, with wild gray hair and wire-rimmed spectacles, casually dressed in jeans and a sweater. He led me to one of the comfy chairs and insisted I join him in a glass of amaretto.

"I work for a liquor distributor, and I like to hear people's opinions on our wares."

The liqueur was excellent and I told him I'd highly recommend it.

He smiled gently. "It's good to have someone to share it with. This house has been pretty lonely without Chris. I haven't had a serious relationship since he died. Or a nonserious one." His lips quirked up slightly with this feeble attempt at humor.

"I visited with his aunt Alida this afternoon." I held up the camera bag I'd carried in with me. "She sent this to you."

"Chris's bag? Where did she get it?"

"Found it in the wheel well of his car. She said she'd been meaning to give it to you."

"I'm glad to have it. Was there anything important in it?"

"Some photographs." I took them from my purse and he thumbed through them.

"Nature shots," he said. "Not terribly inspired. That happened with Chris sometimes when he had an assignment that didn't thrill him. These were probably commissioned by some travel magazine or maybe his newspaper."

"I think it was the paper."

"Well, even an artist like Chris has to take the little jobs to earn a living."

"Do you happen to recognize where those were taken?"

He flipped through them again. "Could be anyplace around here. There's no date stamp, so he must've developed them himself."

"Where?"

"At the newspaper lab. We don't have space here for a darkroom."

"There aren't any negatives."

"Then the paper must have them. I'm not conversant with the legalities, but I assume if they commissioned the photos they have a right to both them and the negatives."

"If it's all right with you, let's not tell them we have them just yet."

"Or ever."

He got up and poured me more amaretto, as if he was afraid our words had ended our visit.

"Do you know what happened to his Leica?" he asked.

"It's still in official hands, Alida said, but once it's returned, it will also go to you."

His brown eyes grew moist. "A nice lady, Alida. A kind lady."

He spoke the word "kind" as if it was one he didn't hear a lot. Come to think of it, neither did I.

"Tell me about Christopher," I said, settling back into my chair.

"What specifically?"

"Nothing specifically. Just tell me who he was."

Over the next hour we discussed his dead partner, me asking many of the questions I would in a formal interview. Chris had been kind, to grown-ups, to children, to animals. He'd been generous to aspiring photographers who wanted advice. He'd often go away for periods of two to three days, but Clive hadn't worried about him. In time he'd return and rush to the newspaper lab to develop his film, then gleefully show off the good shots.

Clive said, "I thought all of them were good, but Chris was a perfectionist."

"Did he have any other interests besides photography?" I asked.

"Classical music; we had season tickets to the symphony. We both volunteered for the Humane Society, collected for the Cancer Society and Heart Association—that sort of stuff. But Chris's true passion was his photography."

He told me nothing that helped the investigation, but I came away with the knowledge of what a truly good man Christopher Wickens had been. Clive Canfield too.

11:30 p.m.

I drove back to my motel, updated my notes, and treated myself to a long, hot bath. While in the tub I called Rae, who as usual was wide awake in spite of the hour.

"Just a sec," she said. "Let me save this." A couple of clicks and she was back to me.

"Working?" I asked.

"I had this idea for a new novel... Well, you'll see—eventually."

"Have you been to visit Ma again?"

"Yes. I spent most of the afternoon there. She was pretty out of it. Hasn't been knitting any more, which is probably just as well."

"Why?"

"Yesterday she started a sweater, only she wasn't doing too good a job of it. I can't imagine who it's supposed to be for; if she ever finishes it, it'll be very big, with long arms that wouldn't fit anybody except an ape. Oh, and the caregiver I arranged for her went by to get acquainted this afternoon and they got along fine."

"Does the caregiver have long arms?"

"What? Oh, I get it. It's late and I'm kind of dense. Anyway, your mom will be going home as soon as she's able."

"I still think I should see her. I'm down in San Luis Obispo—I'll explain why later—and I could swing over to Pacific Grove on the way back—"

"No." Rae's voice was firm. "She made it definite that she doesn't want to see you. Don't know why, but those were her orders. Maybe it's something to do with your other family."

My "other family" and our tangled roots, the lies and half-truths that had been spoon-fed to me since my birth; thank God we'd untangled them and finally spoken the whole truth.

"I don't think that's it," I said. "In fact, Ma and Saskia are good friends. And surely you remember that episode when she concocted an imaginary romance with Elwood. Let's face it, she's just nuts."

"Not everybody who doesn't get on with you is nuts,

Shar. I'm not getting on with you at the moment, and I'm not nuts—just tired. And I'm going to bed." She broke the connection.

I smiled as I switched off my phone. Rae has always been able to put me in my place when I need it.

SATURDAY, AUGUST 13

Acall from Hy woke me from my restless sleep—
brave man—for two reasons. One was to ask me
what if anything I'd learned in the San Luis area, which
wasn't much so far. The second was to ask when I'd be
coming back to the city.

"Why?" I tried to lean against the pillows, but they
were scattered on the floor. I hate sleeping in motel
beds.

"Just missing you. Plus things're getting interesting
here."

"Oh?"

"Tyler Pincus, the amateur magician from the
Breakers, is back in town. Last night KOFY-TV had
a clip of him on the late news, doing a weird dance
in front of the Breakers. He told the reporter he'd
had a vision of a murder there while in an 'elliptacoid
trance.'"

"What the hell is an 'elliptacoid trance'?"

"There's no such thing; I googled it. But from what
Pincus was photographed doing it involves running
around outdoors calling attention to himself and wearing all white with a red sash. The guy's a nutjob."

"Is he still at the Breakers?"

"Maybe, but I think he's kind of lost his audience. So when are you coming home?"

"Later today, probably. I've got one more thing I want to check on here. I'll let you know when I'm on my way."

10:30 a.m.

Santa Marta Creek—population 3,293—was in the foothills of the Santa Lucia Range northeast of Bakersfield. A well-paved highway led me there from San Luis. Nestled between tall stands of ponderosa pines, it consisted of one long block of commercial establishments—laundromat, IGA grocery store, Lil's Coffee Shop, Trekker's Shoes and Sporting Shop, the Rod and Tackle Depot—interspersed with modest homes. I located the county sheriff's substation and, as a courtesy to let them know I would be operating in the area, went inside, where I was greeted by the deputy, Andy Owens. Not all law enforcement people are cordial to private investigators, but he was. He poured me a cup of chicory-flavored coffee, seated me in a comfortable armchair in his otherwise sparsely furnished office, and asked, "So what brings you here from the big, bad city, Ms. McCone?"

"A hunch."

"Not a wild one, I hope. The damn things don't want to let you get off."

A comedian—but the old joke *was* pretty funny, or would have been in different circumstances.

I placed the prints from Chris Wickens's camera bag on the desk. "Does this terrain look familiar to you?"

"Sure does. They must've been taken at Wingspread, the old Reynolds place. I'd recognize that footbridge anywhere. But these shadowy areas—are those people?"

"I think so."

He nodded as if I'd confirmed something he already knew, and absently began hand rolling a cigarette. After a moment he said, "This state, particularly in the wilderness areas, generates a lot of legends. Have you heard of the Dark Watchers?"

"I don't believe I have."

"Folks say they appear either at dawn or dusk. Huge silhouettes that, once sighted, vanish before your eyes. Some describe them as wearing wide-brimmed hats; other claim they carry walking sticks. The only consensus is that they're featureless."

"When was this supposed to have happened?"

"From roughly thirteen thousand years ago to this very day. At least that's how far back the Chumash Indian stories go. The Indians called them 'Los Vigilantes Oscuros.'"

"And you say you recognize the photos as having been taken at a place called Wingspread?"

"It's an old hacienda built by Spanish settlers sometime in the 1800s and passed along until the family died out. Then it was turned into a winery, abandoned now. Maybe ten years ago a young couple name of Krist bought it with the idea of restoring it. They got a start on it too, but then they were killed in a mudslide—damn thing just pushed their car over the cliff near Big Sur. A relative someplace back east inherited it, but hasn't shown any interest. So there it sits."

"Were the Krists renovating it themselves?"

"Not completely. At least, some construction company put up signs, but their workers weren't there long."

"Do you remember the name of the company? Were they local?"

"Sorry, but I don't."

"Would anybody mind if I explored the property?"

"Not if the deputy sheriff gives you permission." His eyes twinkled, then became serious. "I'd be careful, though. A young man—a photographer from the San Luis paper—got himself killed out there a number of years back."

"Christopher Wickens. I've talked with his family."

"Sad case: he was stabbed to death. Body was found on the southwest side of the property, where it drops off into sheer cliff. He was supposed to be taking pictures of the winery, but we guessed he went over there for some shots that would put the place in context."

"You mean, so it could be located in terms of the sea, mountain ridges, and so forth."

"Right."

"Who found the body?"

"Hiker, about a day later." The deputy shook his head. "There was an indication the murder might be linked to other cases in the area. Chris's body was disfigured."

I knew the answer, but I asked, "How?"

"There was something weird carved up high on his chest—a circle within a circle and a funny kind of arrow. Reminded me of drawings you see of the evil eye."

11:35 p.m.

Following the directions Deputy Andy Owens had given me, I took a graveled road up into the Santa Lucias for almost ten miles, then turned onto a dirt track leading still higher. When I stopped at a turnout to look out over the valley, I could see all the way to San Luis and the sea. The air was cooler here and very still; the only thing that moved was a red-tailed hawk that soared overhead and vanished beyond the next ridge. Then there was a scuttling in the brush and a family of quail strutted by, heads bobbing.

I got back into the car and pressed the button for the retractable roof; might as well catch a few rays while I could.

The dirt track continued on, past manzanita and stunted cacti, for two more miles before ending at the massive iron gates to the old winery. They stood ajar, one leaning on a broken hinge. I parked in the shade of a buckeye tree and continued on foot, pulling the gates closed behind me. The ground was rutted from runoff from last winter's rains, but I saw no evidence that a vehicle had passed recently. Around a sharp turn, the track split and curved back to meet itself around a sun-browned patch of land that might once have been a lawn. In a copse of half-dead eucalypti the remains of two picnic tables lay on the ground.

The entire area was surrounded by a rusted chain-link fence, probably left over from the days when the winery had been under renovation. On a couple of wooden signs, affixed near its top, the word "Construction" appeared in faded blue paint, but the signs gave no name for the company. An old yellow tractor stood near the copse of trees, and an earthmover sat near the ruined picnic tables, its jaws frozen open as if it were prepared to take a final bite.

The face of the winery was fieldstone and redwood, but many of the beams were rotten, and the large stones between them had fallen loose. Bright-green moss lurked in the shadows, but where it was exposed to the sun it was dull orange. Terra-cotta tiles had fallen from the winery's roof and were smashed on the ground. From somewhere inside the structure came a steady banging noise—probably a broken shutter moving in the light breeze. I approached the building cautiously, my hand on the butt of my .38; I'd transferred it from my bag to a light holster clipped onto my belt.

I went through weathered double doors into what had once been a tasting room. Dark in there, except for shafts of light that streamed through the places where the roof tiles were missing. Dust motes danced in the beams. I took out my flashlight, shone it around.

Cobwebs. Spiderwebs. Paneling sagging off the walls. Broken mosaic floor tiles. A tasting bar, minus equipment such as sinks and a dishwasher; the back-bar mirror was smashed, and the ornate cornice usually found in such establishments had been torn from its anchoring, probably carted off by vandals. Something moved to my right, and I shone my light that way; a rat, half as big as a jackrabbit, ran across the floor.

A swinging door opened at the right side of the bar. I pushed through it. Beyond was a room filled with oak barrels, their odor musty and pungent. I walked among them. Zinfandel, cabernet, merlot; the dates grease penciled on them were over eight years old. I turned the stopcocks on a few, found them dry.

Okay, this was the winery, but where had the owners and help lived? There was a back door off the barrel room, and I passed through it to the outside. More tall weeds, stunted trees, and a couple of outbuildings, their once-white paint flaking off. I went to the larger of the two.

Bunk beds for eight, their thin mattresses almost devoured by mice. A wood stove. A big round table and rudimentary kitchen cabinets and counters. Through a window I glimpsed a privy.

I felt as if I'd stepped into an episode of *Gunsmoke*.

The smaller building was a house, in marginally better shape than the bunkhouse. Its porch steps teetered as I mounted them. Inside it was fully furnished: Pull-out sofa close to the woodstove; lamps on end tables beside it; a couple of rockers. A bookcase, its paperback volumes also ravaged by mice. I glanced at the titles: the Krists had been into science fiction and astronomy. Well, what better place to study the stars than here, where there was no light pollution?

The adjoining kitchen contained jelly glasses, apparently used for drinking; a few plates that I remembered from my childhood as being called Melmac; miscellaneous flatware, knives, and utensils. A couple of jugs of Carlo Rossi red sat in a bottom cabinet; it was a wonder nobody had appropriated them. (Or maybe not such a wonder.) The bathroom looked as if someone had rushed off to work: towels hanging crookedly on racks, toothbrushes propped on the porcelain, toothpaste stains in the sink. A makeshift closet was crammed with jeans, T-shirts, and sandals.

The house looked as if the couple had planned to return soon, probably would have except for the freak accident that had taken their lives. The items here were largely impersonal. What about things of significance, such as documents, financial records, and correspondence?

Nothing like that on the premises. The Krists must have kept their important papers in a safe-deposit box, but I couldn't locate a key. There were some receipts from Dom's Grocery in Santa Marta Creek—vanilla yogurt, lemons, apples, granola, greens. A healthy diet to go with the wine they'd bought, a good-quality label that maybe they'd been hoping to emulate. Postcards attached by magnets to the fridge door were from the Grand Canyon, Martha's Vineyard, New Orleans, and Dallas. None of the signatures meant anything to me, and the messages were strictly of the "wish you were here" variety. There were few photographs except the kind of formal poses taken for graduations and other landmark occasions. I studied them. Mrs. Krist had been a large woman with thick black eyebrows and a pugnacious jaw. Her bespectacled husband reminded me of a malnourished laboratory assistant.

Finally, tucked partially under a place mat on the cluttered dining table, I found something of interest—an unfinished letter to someone named Nadia, written in a woman's hand. Lots of exclamation points and the *i*'s dotted with little hearts. In an amusing manner it detailed an uneventful day-to-day existence and aired a few dissatisfactions with "the huz," but then the tone became serious.

We've had to shut down the renovation efforts—temporarily, we hope. Two members of the crew went into town on Saturday night and never came back. I think they may have stolen my Visa card because I can't find it anywhere and I've had a devil of a time canceling it. And I'm worried about that guy I told you about who's been acting weird. I can't help feeling something bad is going to happen. Spooky here now. I wish we'd never

The letter ended there.

"Spooky here"—in what way?

And "that guy" Mrs. Krist had been worried about—who was he, and in what way had he been acting weird?

I rummaged through a drawer in the table and came up with a small address book. Leafed through it looking for someone named Nadia. There it was—Nadia Johanssen, 132 Merriwell Street, Camden, Ohio.

There didn't seem to be anything more to look at here, and I was anxious to get back to the city. The San Luis part of the investigation had been fruitful, but I had the germ of an idea about Zack Kaplan's murder and Chelle's disappearance, and if I was right, the answers were back in San Francisco.

I pocketed the unfinished letter and headed for the iron gates. My car was littered inside and out with buckeye leaves, and I scolded myself for having put the top down.

As I turned onto the road, I took one last look at the winery. Spooky, yes. I seldom used the word, but it was appropriate for the place.

6:30 p.m.

Before I started the long, boring drive back to San Francisco I tried calling the number listed for Nadia Johanssen in Camden, Ohio, but it was no longer in service after seven years. So then I called Mick, but the call went to his voice mail. Out somewhere or too busy to answer calls. I left a message asking him to see if he could track down the Johanssen woman's current whereabouts and contact information.

A heavy, stationary mist lay over the city when I finally arrived. It was particularly thick in the Marina, blurring familiar landmarks and masking the lights of other vehicles until they were nearly upon me. I nearly missed the driveway of my own house—an off-white Spanish Revival on a large corner lot. I loved the house: its spaciousness, the light that entered through the many vaulted windows, the arches that allowed one room to flow into another. We'd furnished it in contemporary casual, with area rugs to protect the intricate parquet floors, and added tiles handcrafted by a friend to the bathrooms and kitchen, to replace the badly worn ones that dated from 1915, the year the Panama-Pacific International Exposition had been held nearby.

I stowed my car in the garage and went inside. Hy was at the kitchen table drinking coffee. He got up as I came in, engulfed me in one of his bear hugs. I filled him in on my visit to the old winery, showed him the letter I'd found.

"That mention of a person she was worried about might be a lead," he said, "depending on what she meant by 'acting weird.'"

"I've been thinking the same thing. I'm hoping Nadia Johanssen can provide the details, if she's still alive and locatable."

"Mick will find out. Oh, I recorded the Pincus footage on KOFY. Want to see it?"

"Yes."

He flicked the TV set on. A city official whom I didn't recognize—politicians have all begun to look alike to me—was calling Pincus "another amusing San Francisco character." Next a brief clip appeared of a tall, rail-thin man dressed all in white with a red sash, cavorting in front of the old hotel. Tyler Pincus during his thirty seconds of fame.

"God," I said, sitting down at the table, "this city is turning into a lunatic asylum."

"*Turning* into?"

"More of one."

Truth be told, San Francisco and its residents have always been, to put it gently, a bit off-center: The gold rush, the Barbary Coast, and the robber barons; tong wars and labor strikes; flower children and religious cults; out-of-control housing costs and the homeless. Murder and mayhem at city hall; suicides from both bridges; protest marches and provocateurs. In my years here, I've seen naked men proclaiming their right to be naked in public; the Sisters of Perpetual Indulgence, pseudonuns on roller skates; dancing pandas; socialites riding camels down Van Ness Avenue to raise money for charity; the mayor playing the donkey in a game of pin-the-tail-on.

It's been interesting. I really love this city—its past, its present, and whatever outlandish things its future will bring.

SUNDAY, AUGUST 14

12:10 p.m.

We read the Sunday paper, and I made French toast. Just after we finished eating, I heard from Mick. He'd found Nadia Johanssen, alive and well and now living in Virginia. When I called the number he gave me, a landline answering machine picked up. More frustration. I explained in my message who I was and why I wanted to speak with her, and asked for a callback at her earliest convenience.

Hy left for the office, citing paperwork. I suspected he felt antsy, being cooped up and waiting for something to happen. Well, I was too, so I decided to drive out to the Breakers and see if I could round up Tyler Pincus and find out what had caused his outburst.

The old hotel matched the gray of the afternoon. A strong wind whipped the waves into a frenzy and blew sand from the dunes, peppering its already pockmarked exterior. Pincus wasn't in sight—no one was, except for a solitary dog walker. I approached him and asked if he or anyone he knew had witnessed last night's performance. He had, he said, and while his cocker spaniel licked my fingers and flopped its long ears around my hands, he described a bizarre dance that had culminated in a cacophony of grunts and howls.

"Scared the hell out of Buffy here," he ended.

After the man resumed his walk, I went up and tried the front door. Locked again, but I had the key Cap'n Bobby had given me. Inside, all was chill and silent. I went up and knocked on the door to Pincus's apartment anyway. No answer.

I thought about picking the lock on the door, a fairly easy task judging by the ancient lock, and having a look inside. But there didn't seem to be much point in it. It was Pincus himself I wanted to see.

No telling where he was and what he was up to. Unless maybe he'd taken his crazy magician act to Danny's Inferno, being another habitué of the place. I drove over there to check, since it was close by.

Pincus wasn't there, but Ollie Morse was. Sitting by himself in a small, dark corner booth. Two empty Budweiser bottles were lined up, ready to be taken away, and a fresh one sat in front of him.

I slid into the other side of the booth. "Hey, Ollie," I said. "Where's your buddy?"

"Al? I don't know." He shrugged glumly. "Or much care."

"Something the matter between you two?"

"Nah. He just hands me a pain sometimes, is all."

"Well, how're *you* doing, Ol?"

"Not so good."

"What's wrong?"

"Just the blues. I get them a lot." He swigged beer, then wagged the bottle. "I thought a few brews would help, but not so far."

I didn't tell him to go easy; he knew he should, but

given his war-induced condition, knowing and acting on the premise were two different things.

"I guess Al told you about my PTSD," he said. "I have these hallucinations. Like today, I keep flashing back to the field hospital in Kunar Province after the Battle of Ganjgal where I took the grenade hit." He shuddered. "Was bad. Real bad. Opened up my right side, shattered my ribs, broke my arm." He cradled his left elbow. "The pain was something fierce."

"Do you feel pain during the flashbacks?"

"Sometimes I do—or I think I do."

"Do you have any warning that you're about to have one?"

"Yeah, there's a tingling in my hands and feet, little white lights sparkling like stars."

Pamela Redfin appeared without having been summoned, bringing two bottles of Budweiser. "From Danny and me," she said. "Hi, Sharon. Any news about Chelle?"

I shook my head. "Have you seen Tyler Pincus today?"

"No, and I'm glad of it. You hear about his latest performance?"

"Saw a replay of it on TV."

"He keeps getting weirder and weirder. D'you think he's dangerous?"

"I doubt it. Likely just an exhibitionist."

"A totally whacked exhibitionist, if you ask me."

After she returned to the bar, Ollie said, "I wonder if that's the kind of thing they say about me. Getting weirder, I mean."

"Why would they? You don't dance in the streets."

He smiled faintly. "Well, sometimes I get...a little strange when I have a flashback."

"Does alcohol help you keep from having one?"

"Sometimes yes, sometimes no. I just happen to like beer. Me and Al, Danny calls us the Beer Brothers."

"You and Al must've been friends a long time."

"Since we joined up in our unit. His tour was over a few months before mine. After he mustered out he came here and started up his construction company. We stayed in touch, and when I got out he took me in with him part-time. Got me my apartment in the same building as his so he could watch over me, I guess."

"You still work with him part-time? I thought the two of you were partners."

"Nah. It's Al's business, though I put some money into the shop on Innes. He thinks my spells make me unreliable." The expression on his face said he didn't like being controlled that way. "He's wrong, though," Ollie added. "I'm no more unreliable than the next wage slave. But that's Al—he's always gotta run things his way." He sighed. "Oh, well, he's the one pays for any equipment we might need and the rent on the shop, deals with government forms and stuff like that. I guess he's entitled."

Still, he looked disturbed. He picked up his beer, drank a little, made a face, and put the bottle down again. "Damn beer doesn't taste good any more. Look, I gotta get outta here, get some fresh air. You staying?"

"For a while."

He nodded curtly and slid out of the booth.

3:31 p.m.

After Ollie left, I asked Pamela to substitute a cold glass of Chardonnay for the warm beer. I sat sipping it, staring into the glass. A dark feeling had stolen over me all of a sudden, as if a bad weather front were moving in. Why? I couldn't explain it.

Pamela said, "Are you okay?"

I shook my head: *Yes, no, I don't know.*

"You want me to get Danny over here?"

"No need." The sense of foreboding kept hanging over me...

I'd been sitting there for about ten minutes when my phone buzzed. Rae.

"Shar," she said in a subdued voice, "I'm afraid I've got bad news. There's no way to say it except straight out: your mom passed away suddenly this afternoon."

Her words hit me like a jolt of electricity. In its aftermath I couldn't think. I shook my head to clear it. My voice, when I could make it work, was wooden. "When? How?"

"About twenty minutes ago, just before I got to the hospital." At the same time the dark, oppressive feeling had come over me. "The doctor wanted to be the one to notify you, but I told him it would be better if you heard it from me." She paused and then said, "It was very peaceful, while she was in bed napping. She was just...worn out, I guess."

"I'll come down there—"

"No, don't. There's nothing you can do here now."

"But the arrangements..."

"Don't worry about those now. Deal with that issue

later. Do you want me to notify John, Patsy, and Charlene?"

"No, I'll do it."

"One other thing I need to tell you is that she left a letter for you. Are you home now?"

"I will be soon."

"I'll have it delivered to your house by special messenger."

Oh, God, what kind of message was Ma sending me posthumously?

After we disconnected, I sat feeling numb. I'd experienced other losses, of course, among them my adoptive father and my brother Joey, who had overdosed in a shack in Humboldt County. My best friend from high school, Linnea Carraway, had died in a helicopter crash in Alaska, and *Chronicle* reporter J. D. Smith had been murdered while working on one of my cases. Matty Wildress, Hy's close friend and my flight instructor, had been killed in an air show while we watched from the ground. But Ma...

As Rae said, she had been special, the heart and soul of our family. She had already borne John and Joey, but she didn't hesitate to take me in when Saskia couldn't support me, and then proceeded to expand the family with Charlene and Patsy. Although we never had much money, she made life's trials an adventure for us, such as when a sonic boom from nearby NAS Miramar cracked our small backyard swimming pool; the navy wouldn't pay to repair it, so she had a truckload of soil brought in and planted a vegetable garden that supplied not only us but many of our neighbors. When she divorced Pa, who had more or less stopped noticing her over the years, and married wealthy Melvin Hunt—whom we called King of the Laundromats—she remained the same down-to-earth person, only with a better hairdo. And when Melvin died, she moved from San Diego to Pacific Grove on the Monterey Peninsula, where she took up watercolor painting. Her work was good, and she'd had a couple of local shows.

It was this past Christmas season that I'd started noticing little cracks and flaws in her already quirky personality, among them her fixation on her "romance" with Elwood Farmer. Saskia, with whom Ma had become close, noticed too. But then the fixation disappeared and Ma covered up for it with a tale that convinced me she should have been a fiction writer. When she returned to Pacific Grove after the holidays, I'd assumed she'd again take up her painting and her active social life.

Well, I'd been wrong. And now she was gone.

How do you come to terms with it when a person with whom you've had a very conflicted relationship dies? Do you let go of all the old resentments and guilt? Think, "Well, she didn't mean what she said"? Think, "Well, I didn't mean what I said either"? Or do you gather the bad feelings about you, pick and gnaw at every bone of contention? Do you cling to them because it's the only way to keep the sorrow at bay? Which way would I deal with Ma's death after this numbing fog dissipated?

I'd just have to wait and see…

4:45 p.m.

I posed the same questions to Hy after giving him the sad news. He'd offered as much comfort as he could, holding me, and now, seated at the kitchen table, he took both my hands in his. The cats, ever sensitive to their people's feelings, wound around my legs, brushing their faces against me.

"Everybody's different in how they deal with something like this," he said. "When Julie died"—his first wife, environmentalist Julie Spaulding—"initially I was relieved because her suffering was over."

Julie had suffered from multiple sclerosis and was confined to a wheelchair most of her life. She hadn't let her illness stop her, however, and with money she'd inherited from her father, a big Kern County lettuce grower, she'd established a foundation to provide backing to various environmental organizations. When she'd died, her will had named Hy director of the foundation, and he still sat on its board.

Hy said, "I'd always been wild, as you well know, but Julie was a steadying influence on me; when I lost her, I was angry and out of control. Until you came into my life."

I squeezed his hands.

"I'm not saying it's the same for everybody," he added. "Right now you're grieving, but you also feel regretful because you and your mom didn't get along very well. Next, you may feel guilty because you didn't go down there to see her. Or you may feel angry with her for not wanting you there. With complicated relationships like yours, you never know."

"I already feel guilty. For not going down there and not making more of an effort to resolve the conflict between us. I always thought there'd be time…"

"And probably your mom did too. Maybe this letter Rae's forwarding will make things clearer."

MONDAY, AUGUST 15

9:50 a.m.

The letter from Ma was delivered by special messenger in the morning. I sat down at the kitchen table and read it, then handed it wordlessly to Hy.

After a moment he said, "I wonder if she wrote something like this to your brother and sisters?"

"Rae said only to me. I was adopted, the outsider in the family, you know."

"Did you feel like an outsider?"

"No. I just felt...different."

"It sounds as if she was trying to emphasize once and for all that you weren't an outsider. She may even have been trying to tell you that you were her favorite child."

"She had a strange way of acting on it. She was always riding me about one thing or another."

"I understand that's what people do to their favored ones."

I took the letter from him and read it again. The most meaningful words and phrases stood out.

You were such a lively baby, you brightened our world....The best thing that ever happened to us....Such good grades and such drive to succeed....Sorry about all the lies we told you about your parentage, but at the time it seemed best....I didn't express much appreciation of your choice of career; it seemed too dangerous...but every time I heard about you solving one of your cases, I was so proud of you, honey.

This and the rest of what she'd written would remain with me the rest of my life.

My eyes stung with tears, the first time I'd been able to cry since receiving Rae's call. "This letter is in Rae's handwriting. Ma dictated it to her. That means she knew she was going to die soon, but she made the effort anyway."

"All the more reason to treasure it."

I folded the letter and put it in my shirt pocket, feeling drained. I'd spent the evening before notifying friends and relatives who should receive the news, speaking at length with my brother and my sister Patsy, as well as half sister Robin, Saskia, Elwood, Rae, and Hank. Charlene I'd been able to talk to only briefly.

John, with typical stoicism, offered to make the arrangements for Ma's cremation, and said we'd plan a service and scattering of the ashes for a time in the fall when most people could attend. Clearing out the home and selling it could wait awhile. "Do you want me to tell my boys?" he asked.

His two sons from a long-ago marriage, now living back east in Boston and Raleigh, North Carolina. I was glad he offered; I hardly knew my nephews, and I wondered if John really did either.

"If you would," I said.

"I take it Mick knows."

"Rae called him immediately after we talked, and I've been in touch with him all evening."

Patsy, of course, was ever practical, and began talking of a menu for the memorial service. Food has always been her response to crises, but I knew she'd be weeping in her fiancé Ben's arms minutes after we ended the call.

I didn't know or care what time it was in London, and woke Charlene out of a sound sleep. Predictably, she went to pieces. Vic assured me he would get her calmed down.

Elwood and Saskia were calm and resigned; both were private people and kept their sorrows to themselves. Robin, whom I'd always regarded as overly emotional, surprised me by doing the same.

It had been a long, difficult evening after a trying day. Little wonder I was still exhausted. But I couldn't just mope around the house; I'd be climbing the walls before noon if I did that. Chelle was still missing, Zack Kaplan's murderer still unidentified. Those issues were what I had to focus on today, and every day until they were resolved.

11:15 a.m.

Tyler Pincus wasn't at the Breakers. Or at Danny's Inferno. I talked to a couple of the neighbors, but they hadn't seen him that day and had no idea where he might be. Both said they'd be happy if they never saw him again.

12:40 p.m.

Monday-afternoon quiet at the agency. Most operatives out doing—I hoped—their jobs. I spoke briefly with Ted and Patrick, who both offered their condolences about Ma. Will wasn't there; I called him from my office to ask if he'd turned up any new information—he hadn't. I tried Nadia Johanssen's number again, and again got her answering machine. Then I compulsively went over Will's reports and my notes on Chelle's disappearance and the Carver killings. There had to be *something* there that would lead me to the answers, but I couldn't pinpoint it if there was. I went over everything again, with the same lack of results.

Frustration made me get up and pace around like a cat in a cage. After a time I stopped that and sat down in the armchair beneath Mr. T. The cleaning staff must've been in last night; his leaves had been dusted. The chair had once been a horrible, butt-sprung fixture in my office—in actuality, a closet under the stairs—at All Souls. I'd dragged it along with me to Pier 24½, and Ted had spirited it away while I was on vacation and had it reupholstered in a wonderful soft leather. Now I snuggled into it, drew a hand-woven alpaca throw around me, and sat looking out at the Bay and the hills and flatlands without really seeing them.

But the frustration didn't let me stay there for long. Dammit, sitting and brooding wasn't getting me anywhere. I needed to *do* something, even if it proved to be another waste of time.

I got up off my ass, left M&R, and drove once more to the Outerlands.

5:03 p.m.

Fog was rolling in off the Pacific, enveloping Ocean Beach and Jardin Street. No lights were visible inside the Breakers, but I stopped my car and got out anyway. And when I did, I heard a weird wailing in the adjacent alley, accompanied by the slapping of feet.

"Ooohla-ooohla-ump-tha!"

"Rah-rashanti!"

"Ump-tha!"

The voices were different, and at first I thought there were several people chanting, but only one emerged onto the sidewalk. Tall, clad all in white except for a red sash that billowed in the offshore breeze—I'd finally found Tyler Pincus. Apparently, among his other accomplishments, he could speak in tongues.

"Ump-tha! Walla-walla-walla!"

I didn't know exactly what whirling dervishes did, but it seemed an adequate term to describe Pincus's antics. Apparently he'd left the building through the cellar entrance and was on his way someplace to perform magic or wizardry or whatever he did for fun and little profit.

"Ump-tha?" he said when he saw me.

"Walla-walla-walla," I replied.

He looked shocked. "Who're you?"

"A friend and fellow believer."

"So you know of these evil things."

"I do. Are you performing an exorcism?"

"No exorcism. Mourning."

"Mourning whom?"

"The dead one."

"Zack Kaplan?"

"Cut off in the prime of his youth by the evil one."

"Who is the evil one?"

"The dog of many faces and the dead eyes."

"What's his name?"

"He's the one. I know. I know."

"How do you know? Did you see him kill Zack Kaplan?"

"Ump-tha! Ump-tha!"

Oh, Christ, I thought, *I can't deal with this kind of mumbo jumbo. What he needs is a straitjacket. But maybe if I can calm him down, I can get some rational answers out of him. Or the police can.*

I caught his arm to keep him from dancing any more. "You looked tired, Mr. Pincus—"

"Pincus the magician. Pincus the grand wizard."

"Why don't you sit in my car and relax for a while?"

"Your car?" He peered around. "Oh, red!" And made a beeline for it.

I stayed where I was and called the SFPD. This time I reached Jamie Strogan. "I'm with Tyler Pincus," I said. "You know who he is."

"The loony magician who's been making a spectacle of himself."

"Loony, yes, but he's been talking as if he knows something about the Kaplan homicide."

"Where are you?"

"At the Breakers. He's sitting in my car, and I can try to bring him to the Hall of Justice, but he's manic as hell and liable to make a break before I get there."

"Don't even try. I'm about to go off duty and I'll come out there on my way home. Can you hold him there for twenty minutes?"

"I will if I have to tie him up."

"All right. I'm on my way."

I peered into my car. Pincus was fiddling with the sound system. Just as I started over to it, my phone buzzed. Nadia Johanssen, returning my call to her Virginia home.

"I'm sorry I didn't get back to you sooner, Ms. McCone," she said, "but I was out of town over the weekend."

"Not a problem. You are the Nadia Johanssen who corresponded with Dana Krist?"

"Yes, I am. We'd been friends since our freshman year at Bennington. But she and her husband were killed in an accident more than seven years ago. In fact, I was about to fly out to California to see her when I got the news of the accident."

"Any special reason for making the trip?"

"Well, we hadn't seen each other for a long time and, frankly, I was worried about her. I'd gotten a few odd, rambling letters, and she and Hal had been having problems at an old winery they were trying to restore."

Keeping an eye on Pincus, I said, "That's why I

contacted you, Ms. Johanssen. About those problems she and her husband were having. Let me read you a partially finished letter I found at the winery." I did, and then I asked, "What can you tell me about the man who worried her because he was acting weird?"

"Let me think a moment...Oh, yes, it was one of the workmen, a carpenter or something."

"Did she give his name?"

"I don't remember it if she did, and I no longer have her letters."

"In what way was the man acting weird?"

"Being aggressive, making trouble with the other workmen. I think Hal fired him, or was going to. He was a former Special Forces guy, Hal, and he wouldn't put up with that kind of behavior."

"Do you remember anything else Dana might have told you about the trouble?"

She thought about it. "I'm sorry, no. Seven years is such a long time."

"Yes, it is."

I thanked her and ended the conversation. As I put my phone away, Pincus yelled from the car, "No Canned Heat."

"Try Country Joe and the Fish." I was pretty sure the band was on one of the oldies discs I had stored there.

In half a minute the strains of "The Masked Marauder" filtered out to me.

Appropriate.

5:57 p.m.

"Pincus is still in my car," I told Jamie Strogan when he arrived in his unmarked police vehicle. "I found him a brand-new toy—my car's sound system."

"Listening to Mozart, no doubt. What's his story?"

I explained as best I could, although that took some doing to someone who hadn't yet met Pincus.

Jamie asked, "You really think he witnessed a murder?"

"Well, something put the idea in his head."

"I'll see what I can get out of him."

I let Jamie sit beside Pincus, turn off Country Joe and the Fish, and identify himself. I left the passenger door open so I could listen to their conversation.

"Mr. Pincus, I understand you witnessed a murder. When was this?"

"Yesterday."

Jamie raised an eyebrow at me. I nodded. We were both thinking that Zack had been killed several days ago.

"And who was the victim?"

"The dead one."

"Your neighbor, Zack Kaplan?"

"Cut off in his prime by the dog with many faces and the dead eyes."

Here we go again.

"Who's this dog of many faces? What's his name?"

"I have seen him many times. Now and then."

"What's his name, Mr. Pincus?"

"The evil one."

"His name, what's his name?"

At first Pincus hadn't seemed to mind being interrogated by a police officer, but now he began to show signs of agitation. He flipped through the folder where I keep my CDs. "No Canned Heat," he mumbled. "No Canned Heat! No Grateful Dead!" He waved the folder, scattering CDs all over the interior. Then he shoved the door all the way open, nearly knocking me over as he lunged out, and was off and running.

Neither Jamie nor I bothered to give chase. He sighed and said, "Crazy as hell, all right. I doubt he knows anything, but I'll put out a BOLO on him."

"Probably a good idea, for his own safety. But my guess is that he'll turn up here again; the Breakers is his home, and I doubt he has many friends."

After Jamie left, I got into the Mercedes. But I didn't go anywhere yet. It was cold in the car, the offshore winds buffeting it. I turned the key in the ignition and flipped the switch for what Mick calls the "tush toaster." After a few moments, warmth spread through me.

I kept thinking about the conversation with Nadia Johanssen. So the Krists' trouble had been with an aggressive member of their construction crew. Maybe a carpenter, maybe just a general laborer—

Construction. Construction worker.

Damon Delahanty, Chelle's old boyfriend, was one. Al Majewski had had construction jobs before and after his military service. So had Ollie Morse...

Ollie.

Ollie had pale-blue eyes that very often registered nothing at all.

Ollie, who was unstable enough to require supervision and who showed signs of aggressive behavior.

Mentally I replayed what he and I had talked about yesterday afternoon at Danny's Inferno, and before that, here at the Breakers. The grenade attack in Afghanistan. His struggles with PTSD. His bitterness at Al's refusal to let him work full-time, even though Ollie had invested money in the shop on Innes Avenue, because Al thought his friend was unreliable.

Had Ollie lived and worked on the Central Coast before joining the army? If he had, then it was entirely possible he was the Carver.

7:10 p.m.

Ollie wasn't at his apartment on Forty-Seventh Avenue. He wasn't at the Inferno either. The Redfins hadn't seen him since the day before.

Now what?

Well, I could drive to the Innes Avenue shop and see if Ollie and Al were there working late. It was a small chance, but I had nowhere else to look tonight. And despite being tired and hungry, I was reluctant to give up the hunt just yet.

All right, I'd swing by the shop. If Ollie wasn't there, then I'd go on home and start looking for him again tomorrow.

8:00 p.m.

Dusk was gathering, and fog shrouded the shapes of the distant cranes and gantries of the Hunter's Point shipyard. Broken-down railcars stood on a siding, and beyond them the waters of India Basin stretched flat and placid. I pulled my car under the portico of an old forties-style gas station near the intersection of Innes and Third Street. The building was splashed with graffiti and the pumps were long gone; ivy covered the roof.

Hunter's Point and its environs have been in a state of flux for years. Thousands of mostly affordable homes were planned for the area, but its development has been stymied over and over by reports showing toxic soil and groundwater. A 2018 report revealed that much of the data in a US Navy study had been either falsified or misinterpreted as to conditions that can contribute to high rates of asthma and heart attacks, cancer clusters, and toxic hotspots. It's considered one of the most dangerous areas in the city—for both health and criminal reasons. Gunshots ring out nightly; windows are barred against breakage or theft; taggers roam the streets with their spray paint cans, and most of the buildings, inhabited or not, show evidence of their "artwork." Muggings, understandably, are low on the list of crimes; people at the Point don't have much to steal.

Across the potholed pavement from where I'd parked stood Albion Castle. A forbidding six-story stone edifice, the former home of Albion Porter & Ale Brewery, it was built in the 1870s as both a home and a brewery, owing to its underground springs and large cisterns full of pure, fresh water. A long succession of owners have lived there, but tonight its windows were dark and shuttered.

I checked the load in my .38, then stuck it in my belt. Took out my small but powerful flashlight and tucked it into my rear pocket. When I got out, I set the car alarm to maximum.

Innes was not a long street, ending at India Basin. Mostly deserted at this time of night. I moved warily along the dark, short block of businesses, most of which were behind chain-link fences: Zimmer Boatyard; Halvorsen Brothers Marine; X-pert Cargo & Hauling; Long-Term Storage; AM Construction...

AM Construction was small, compared to the businesses to either side. Built of various kinds of scrap lumber—plywood, cheap paneling, particleboard, and two types of aluminum siding—it seemed impermanent. A door opened onto the street, but there were no windows, and when I approached the door I saw a system of padlocks that would have confounded the most skillful of thieves. Now, what could a construction shack hold that would warrant such security?

Sounds startled me: men's voices coming along the street, arguing. I ducked down a narrow alley to the right.

"You says so? You got proof?"

"Don' need no proof."

"That's 'cause there *ain't* any."

"I tell you, it be so."

"Can't be."

"Can so!"

"If I give you a buck for every time you tell me..."

They passed, and their voices faded as they went into a nearby house.

I continued along the side of AM Construction. Trash and broken glass littered the pebbled ground. Tar paper covered the walls here and there, but when I touched it I felt solid wood behind. At the rear, maybe four feet away, another building stood, its lower windows lighted. I slipped close to one and peered through.

A dozen sewing machines, plied by young Asian women in shabby clothing. The machines clacked and hummed as the women deftly fed them brightly colored cloth; at a side table, two others removed more cloth from bolts and cut it into pieces. When one of the sewing workers finished a piece, a third woman delivered the new cloth and collected the finished product. Beside a door at the front of the small, cramped room stood a large man who reminded me of a prison guard. No way out of this sweatshop.

I ducked down below the sweatshop's windows and moved along the back wall of AM Construction, looking for a rear door. There was none, but around the other side I found a small, high window covered in pieces of plywood that were nailed to its frame. In my bag I had just the remedy for this situation: a multiuse tool with an attachment for prying out nails. I looked around, spotted a discarded packing box a few feet away, and dragged it over to the window. I mounted it and attacked the plywood; it splintered and cracked as I pulled. I had no fear of anyone investigating what was going on; such sounds were probably a nightly occurrence in this neighborhood.

Finally the last board over the window gave way.

I peered through the opening. There was no glass in the window frame, and the interior was totally dark. I took out my small flash and shone it around.

The space appeared to be a typical workshop: table with two high-intensity lamps and a vise mounted on either end; pegboard behind it with neat rows of hand tools; power tools in a separate cabinet, each housed within its own compartment. Two sawhorses with a board across them held open paint cans, probably drying so they could be taken to the dump. Various workbenches were folded up and leaned against what looked like a makeshift wall to the right.

At the far end was a closed door to another room or storage closet. The place smelled of sawdust, dampness, and chemical compounds, and the floor was slick with oil.

I moved the light to the center and swept it up and down; three thick support beams lined up there. There was something under the middle one—

A mewling sound, like a sick kitten. But it was a human voice, a woman's voice.

Chelle!

Quickly I pulled myself through the opening, dropped to a concrete floor. The mewling sound came again and I pinpointed it with the flash beam. She was lying on a cushioned mat, a wool blanket draped over her, at the base of the middle support post. When I reached her I saw that her hands were tied around the pole with thick nylon cord, tightly enough that she couldn't move them more than a few inches. Her legs were free, but the position had to be extremely uncomfortable. A blue-and-white dishtowel was tied securely over her mouth.

"It's me, Chelle—Shar. Don't be afraid."

She seemed not to hear me. She looked straight up into the flash's beam, moaned, and then turned her head away.

"Chelle!"

No answer.

I went to work getting her free of her restraints. My multiuse tool had never been more useful. Once I'd cut the nylon cord binding her hands, I rolled her onto her back and checked to see if she was wounded in any way. No, there were no marks on her except for cord burns on her wrists and a few small scrapes and bruises; her clothes were disarranged but not torn. I lifted her into a sitting position with her back against the pole, began gently massaging her wrists.

She came around after a bit, licked her dry, cracked lips. "Water," she whispered, and moved her head to the right. "Please."

Water. The closed door...Could there be a bathroom behind it? I stood and hurried over there. The first thing I saw when I opened the door was an old chemical toilet, but this wasn't a bathroom—just an alcove that was mainly used for storage. No sink. No running water.

I went back to Chelle.

"Please. So thirsty..."

Did I have anything in my bag that would slake her thirst? No. Not even a tube of ChapStick for her dry, cracked lips.

"Water," she whispered again. "Behind wall."

God, was she delirious? She still didn't seem to recognize me.

"Puddles."

Puddles? What the hell did that mean?

"Chelle, what puddles?"

"Behind the wall. He told me about them." Her voice was stronger now. Good sign.

"What wall?"

"Over there." She jerked her head toward the makeshift wall with the workbenches leaning against it.

And then I remembered the underground aquifer and the cisterns that could be reached by a cave entrance at Albion Castle.

"Be right back," I said.

I followed my flashlight's beam along the floor to the makeshift wall. It had been built where the concrete ended, was constructed of the same disparate materials as the exterior of the building, and stretched between another row of support beams. There was no door in it, but I found a loose board at the far end. When I pulled it free, there was just enough room for me to squeeze through to the other side.

The ground there was mostly mud pockmarked by a half-dozen small puddles of water. Apparently the brewery's cisterns leaked, and the water seeped under the adjoining warehouses and in here.

What to put it in? I had nothing that could hold liquid. I reached into my bag and my fingers touched cloth—a headscarf I kept there for bad weather. I pulled it out, shone the light on it. Dirty.

What the hell, she's been through this much—a little dirt won't hurt her.

I soaked the scarf in one of the puddles and hurried back to her. Propped her head on my arm and held the scarf to her lips. She sputtered, mumbled in protest, tried to push me away.

"Chelle, it's water," I said. "Fresh water from the springs." I thrust the scarf at her mouth and she began to suck on it.

It took three more trips to the seepage before Chelle had ingested enough water that she could sit up on her own. She looked me in the face, her eyes finally showing recognition.

"Shar," she said. "Oh, Shar, thank God you found me."

"It's going to be all right now."

She rubbed her upper arms, wincing. "Sore," she muttered in a rough voice, "So sore."

"Poor circulation. It'll go away soon. How long have you been tied up in here?"

"Don't know. Out of it most of the time."

"Drugged?"

"...Yes."

"Why did he bring you here? What was he planning to do to you?"

She shook her head, her tongue flicking over her lips again.

"More water?" I asked.

"No. Might puke."

"No puking allowed," I said inanely; I was trying to think of a way to get her out of there. I'd need more help than she could give me.

"Can you stand?" I asked her.

"...Try." She flopped her arm around my shoulders and I helped lift her upright. Her knees immediately gave out. I eased her back down onto the cushioned mat.

"All right. Keep trying to restore circulation. I'm going to call for help. I doubt you can navigate the way I came in, and the door's padlocked."

"Okay."

No signal when I tried to call 911. Damn! This must be one of the city's dead spots. I hurried over to the window, boosted myself up, and dropped to the ground outside. I got a clear signal out there and made the call asking for an ambulance as well as the police.

Then I decided to reconnoiter. It was full dark now, but I didn't want to use my flash, so I crept forward, feeling my way along the building's side. It had gotten cold, as August nights will do here in the city. What few streetlights hadn't been vandalized were dim. In the distance I could hear traffic noises and the wail of sirens from the hospital complex a few miles away.

Male voices from down the street, quarreling. Probably the guys who had passed by earlier. Downhill, brakes were screeching, horns honking. I heard the pop-pop-pop of fireworks. Babies were crying, a woman yelling, powerful engines revving. Car coming...

I'd arrived at the front of the building by now, and I risked a look around it. An old, noisy white truck. It turned uphill and parked in front of the shop. A tall man got out and started working the locks on the door.

I ran back to the window, boosted myself inside, and whispered Chelle's name. No reply, and I couldn't find her with the light. The ropes she'd been tied with lay in a tangle on the ground; she must have become frightened and hidden herself somewhere. But where, in her weakened condition?

Locks clicked outside the door. A chain rattled. I

took out my .38, held it in my right hand, and with my left aimed the flash at the door. When it opened, I switched the beam on.

Yellow eyes flared at me. But not Ollie's eyes.

It was Al.

He dropped the Carl's Jr. bag he carried and dodged to one side, trying to avoid the light. He must have been wearing those yellowish glasses that help you see at night, but the flashlight's glare was too powerful for them to do him any good. He kept shifting his feet around even after I'd steadied the light.

"Hold it there, Al," I said. "I'm armed."

He stopped still. After a few seconds, he asked, "What is this?"

"You know."

"Sharon? That you?"

He glanced over toward where Chelle had been trussed up. The place was wrapped in shadows, invisible from where he stood with the light in his eyes. He couldn't know yet that I'd found her. He took a step forward.

"Stay back!"

"What're you doing here?"

"You know that too."

"What? I come here to my shop and I find you poking around in the dark. How should I know why you're here? Far as I'm concerned, you're guilty of breaking and entering, trespassing."

"Keep it up, Al."

"Keep *what* up? Look, there's no money in the place. No drugs either. I don't get into any of that stuff. I'm just a broken-down construction worker trying to scrape up enough cash for my nightly beer."

I didn't reply. I was listening to my surroundings, trying to figure out where Chelle had gone.

Al took another step toward me. I brought the flash up on his face. His features were chiseled into hard lines, but a corner of his mouth twitched.

"Come on, Sharon," he said, "let's talk this over like reasonable people."

Another step, gliding as if he hoped I wouldn't notice.

"Stop right there!"

His eyes narrowed. He feinted to the right, then to the left. And then he sprang at me.

I sidestepped, but he plowed into my left shoulder and twisted me around, and I stumbled into the sidewall. Recovered my balance and dodged clear. Before he could lunge at me again, I set my feet and fired the .38.

The shot narrowly missed him, froze him in his tracks. The flash wobbled a little in my hand, the beam creating eerie patterns on the wall behind where he stood.

"Give it up, Al!" I shouted. "The next shot won't miss."

"You'll have to kill me first."

"Like you killed all those people on the Central Coast and Zack Kaplan here in the city."

"I don't know what the hell you're talking about."

"You know, all right. Stand still! Don't make me shoot you, Al."

"You can't fire fast enough."

"I'm an expert shot."

"I'll kill *you*, you bitch—!"

"No, you're all through killing people. And all through carving the evil eye into your victims."

He went berserk then, let out a roar that must've strained his throat muscles, yanked something out of his pocket. There was a *snick*, and the flash beam glinted off the long blade of a switch knife. I had no choice then. As soon as he made a move toward me, I shot him in the fleshy part of his thigh.

The impact made him drop the knife, threw him off balance, but didn't knock him down. He staggered away from me, sideways toward the door. But something got in his way before he reached it; there was a crashing sound, another, and then stillness.

I steadied the light and pinned him with it. He'd fallen over the two sawhorses with the plank between them that held open paint cans. He must have banged his head when he fell, for he appeared to be unconscious, his respiration erratic. A smear of blue paint stained the front of his work shirt, a brighter smear of red glistened on his pants leg. My bullet had gone through the fleshy part of his thigh. It hadn't severed an artery, or there would have been more blood. He wouldn't bleed to death before the EMTs showed up.

I took a couple of steps closer to him. That was when I saw that his shirt was ripped at his right shoulder and down his arm, revealing the area below his clavicle. A crudely executed tattoo was visible there— an eye with Medusa-like hair and an arrow piercing through it.

The evil eye, this time on living flesh.

When I was sure he was unconscious, I called out Chelle's name to let her know I was all right and it was safe for her to show herself. Then I picked up the nylon cord Al had used to tie Chelle and tethered his hands behind him. While I was doing that, I heard sounds over by the makeshift wall, then the dragging of bare feet on concrete. Chelle limped up to me and put a hand on my arm. Her hands and clothing were wet and streaked with mud.

"I heard the shot," she said. "Is he dead?"

"No. He'll live to stand trial." I shielded the flash so it didn't shine in her eyes, took a look at her face. "You okay?"

"Sure."

"No, you're not." Her face was milk pale, there were cuts on her forehead and chin, and she cradled her rope-burned right wrist.

"Don't give me that look, Shar," she added. "This is nothing. You should see me after a good game of—" And then she collapsed in my arms.

Where the hell were the police and the ambulance? Late as usual. San Francisco has one of the lowest response rates of any major city in the country. Our medical personnel do a great job—when they get there.

I maneuvered Chelle back onto the mat, held her till she came around again. "Whooo!" she said. "That was weird. I've never fainted before. Al—is he dead? No, you said he wasn't. You know...I can't help but feel a little sorry for him."

"He tied you up in here, was going to kill you. And you feel *sorry for him*?"

"He wasn't going to kill me. At first I thought he was, but he couldn't make up his mind. So then I decided to play confessor. You know—let him work out his demons."

"And did he?"

"He's got too many demons for that." She tried to smile, but the corner of her mouth spasmed.

Stockholm syndrome, I thought, *the captive forming an unwitting bond with the captor. She'll get over it before his trial.*

I asked, "Where were you hiding?"

"Where the puddles are, behind the partition." She shivered, then managed a wan smile. "I drank some more of the water. It's not bad—somebody ought to bottle it."

"They did," I said, "during Prohibition."

"What happened?"

"Prohibition was repealed and everybody went back to booze."

WEDNESDAY, AUGUST 17

1:30 p.m.

I wasn't sure whether Chelle's bandages and dressings made her look better or worse than when she'd crawled out of "the swamp," as she'd taken to calling it.

After two days she still bore the physical marks of her ordeal: bruises and cuts and scrapes and rope burns. But she was in good condition otherwise. The drugs Al had fed her proved to have been tranquilizers that had been prescribed for Ollie and so presented no lasting problems. Neither did the effects of trauma, evidently. She was young and mentally healthy, and her spirits were good. She cheerfully claimed that all the attention from law enforcement and the media made her feel like a celebrity. And she certainly had been glad to see all the well-wishers crowded into her hospital room, the floor attendants having decided to ignore the official two-visitor policy.

Hy and I were the only two there now. A pair of Chelle's friends from the rehabbers' association had just left. Brother John had dropped by earlier, bringing a book of her favorite puzzles. Rae had called and the two of them had chatted for a while; then she'd asked to speak to me.

"I'm coming home tomorrow and bringing you guys a present," she said.

"What? Not one of those ugly Chinese urns Ma collected. I know they're valuable, but they're so damn awful."

"Nope. This is something much nicer."

"Oh?" When Rae takes on her upbeat cheerleader's tone I'm always wary.

"Samuel the cat. He needs a home, but Ricky and I can't take on any more than we've already got. So Samuel is about to become the latest addition to the McCone-Ripinsky household."

"I don't know if Alex and Jessie will accept him."

"Sure they will; he's a sweetheart."

I'd put the phone on speaker, and now Hy raised his eyebrows in helpless surrender.

"Okay," I said with a sigh. "We'll see the two of you when you get here."

Less than a minute later, Ollie Morse entered the room shyly. Chelle patted the chair beside her bed and he sat tentatively, as if he felt he wouldn't be welcome.

Ollie wore rumpled chinos and a sport shirt that was missing two buttons. His pale-blue eyes looked sad and lost. The dog of many faces with the dead eyes. Pincus had meant Ollie, whom he'd seen working at the Breakers, but that business about witnessing him commit murder had been pure delusion. But a fortunate one, or I might not have found Chelle.

When she took Ollie's hand, he brightened some, but I could tell he still felt out of place. "How're you feeling, Ollie?" she asked him.

"Kind of fuzzy." He grinned humorlessly. "But there're a lot of people who think I'm always fuzzy."

Then his mouth turned down. "I just can't understand about Al. I always thought he was one of the good guys. Saved my life in battle, looked out for me after we got back. How could he do all those crazy things and I never had a clue?"

"He was two different people in the same body," Chelle said. "You know, like Jekyll and Hyde."

"Right," I added. "The good part of him was the friend you knew, Ollie, the bad part he kept locked inside him."

He nodded, looked down at his clasped hands.

Ollie had told the police that he'd seen the tattoo on Al's shoulder but hadn't known what it was, and that Al wouldn't talk about it. But Chelle had known when she saw it. Al had taken off his shirt while doing some plumbing, thinking he was alone in the Breakers, and she'd walked in on him and remembered the Carver clipping on the killers' wall. She blurted out, "My God, that's the Carver's symbol!" and he'd flown into a sudden, violent rage and tried to grab her. She'd managed to get away from him and run.

She was in such a panic she didn't know what to do. She did try to get hold of me, and when she couldn't she should have gone straight to the police. She hadn't because she didn't trust them and was afraid they wouldn't believe her. "A leftover kid thing," she'd said. "Pretty stupid, huh?"

She remembered Billy Clyde and started out to the airport with him, thinking of going to her folks in Costa Rica. But he'd driven a weird route out by Hunter's Point and taken all the money she had. She jumped out of the van and went to her friend Ginny's house because it was nearby, but Ginny didn't have any money either. The only place she could think of to go then was home. But Al had had the same idea and found her hiding. Instead of killing her, he'd trussed her up and driven her to the shop on Innes. He'd kept her tied up there except when he allowed her to eat and use the toilet, not letting Ollie go near the shop the entire time.

He seemed conflicted about what to do with Chelle; that was why he'd brought the mat, blanket, and food for her. Once she'd gotten her fear and her wits under control, she'd taken advantage of his uncertainty and got him talking about himself. And eventually convinced him to let her write the note to Zack. She'd told him it was so it would seem she'd disappeared voluntarily, but her real purpose was to include a code word that she and her folks had made up as an alert if any of them found themselves in danger. But Al insisted on dictating the single "right to disappear" line and wouldn't let her add anything else.

He'd gone to the Breakers that night and slid the note under the door to Zack's apartment. Somehow Zack must have seen him, and, after making that excited phone call to me, foolishly confronted him while he was still in the building. Al either killed and branded him right there or did it in the vacant lot where the body was found. And it had been Al who'd removed the Carver clipping from the killers' wall, that night or the next day.

Ollie said, "I guess I understand about Al being two different people. But what made him start killing all those people?"

"According to what he told me," Chelle said, "it was

all wrapped up with his lousy, poverty-stricken child-hood and the evil eye."

"How so?"

"His father had a belt with a metal evil eye upraised on it. He used to beat Al with it. Finally Al struck back and his father overpowered him, tied him down, and tattooed the symbol on his shoulder. He was an illiterate drunk who also abused Al's mother, and she committed suicide when Al was fourteen."

One of the American families who live in poverty, ig-norance, and, yes—in hell. Where are the solutions to this? Where are the people who can create such solu-tions?

"Jesus. Al never said a word to me about any of that. Just that he ran away from home when he was a kid, made his way down here, and started working construction soon as he was old enough." Ollie shook his head. "What about his victims—what did they do to him?"

"That's where it gets really weird. He claimed each of them had given him the evil eye and de-served to die and be branded with one. Chelle tried to get him to tell her what giving the evil eye con-sisted of, but then he went really out of whack, said she couldn't understand because she didn't have one. I guess that saved her life."

"Did he say anything about doing any evil eye killings when we were in Afghanistan?"

Chelle said, "Not that he'd admit to. He claimed he joined the service to try to stop himself from commit-ting more Carver murders. The only person he admit-ted to killing since is poor Zack."

"D'you think he'd have . . . killed you, finally?"

"I don't even want to speculate on that. Maybe he realized he'd gone too far. He—"

Her phone's ringtone interrupted her. She looked at the screen and said, "It's my folks, finally." This was the first word she'd had from them.

Ollie took that as a signal to depart. Hy and I went out into the hall with him, to give Chelle privacy. As I watched Ollie slouching off toward the elevators, I wondered how he would get along without Al to watch over him. Probably not too well, considering his PTSD, how much he drank, and how lost he seemed. Maybe Hy could get him some professional help; he knew several combat vets and had contacts in the Veterans Administration. I'd talk to him about it later.

While we waited for Chelle to finish her call, I said, "I can't believe the Curleys have been so busy back in D.C. that they couldn't take the time to call her before this."

"Some people are not cut out to be parents," Hy said. "She's always been on her own, doing amazing things for a young person, but with little support from them."

"From what she said about the code word, I guess she knew all along what they were doing. You know, it's amazing how little we know about others, including friends of long standing."

"Ain't it, though..."

A nurse appeared and went into the room. When she came out, she indicated that Chelle was ready for us to go back inside.

Chelle's nose was pink, her eyes red and wet. "It wasn't too great a conversation," she said. "Mom told me they're being debriefed on their latest assignment and then they're gonna come home and 'devote' themselves to me. Is that smothering or what?"

I nodded. "Pretty smothering."

"Anyway, this 'devotion' stuff doesn't shake me up too much. Knowing my folks, they'll get bored after a while even if they don't get involved in some other government job. Dad did have a piece of good advice, though: stop living in the buildings I'm rehabbing. He's right. I'm getting too old to be sleeping on mattresses in half-finished places and eating takeout all the time."

Too old, at the worldly age of twenty-three!

Of course, I hadn't been many years older than that when I bought my first house because I was sick of my studio apartment.

"I'd like to buy here in the city," she said as if she'd read my thoughts, "but property is so pricey. It might take a year or more to find a place I can afford. And I can't live with my parents until I do, not with all the bad memories from when I had to hide there and then got dragged out."

Uh-oh. I can feel it coming.

"I could rent or lease an apartment, I guess, but I'd have to pay a fortune and just be throwing away good money I could be saving."

Chelle frowned at Hy's and my silence, but went on, "You can see the problem. If I could find someplace big enough that I wouldn't be a drag on the other people living there and maybe do chores or something to subsidize my rent..."

She looked so earnest that I tried not to laugh, but the tension of the past weeks welled up.

Hy nudged me. "Our two boarders—Samuel the cat and Chelle."

I clapped my hand over my mouth, trying to repress myself, and snorted—my preliminary response to hysterical laughter.

"Uh-oh," Hy said, and started patting my back.

"Sorry," I gasped, "but it's so..." *Snort!*

Hy said to Chelle, "I can't stop her when she gets this way."

"I can't either..." *Snort!*

"Not you too!"

Snort!

Hy sighed and addressed the absent Samuel the cat. "Life at our house is not going to be easy, pardner, but it sure as hell will be interesting."

And then he snorted too.

SUNDAY, SEPTEMBER 16

7:13 p.m.

We stood on the bluff-top platform at Touch-stone, all of us who had loved Ma. Hy and me, John, Charlene and Vic, Patsy and Ben, Hank and Habiba. Rae and Ricky had come up the night before to help with the preparations for the buffet supper. The grandchildren who were old enough to understand stood with us, and the little ones played on the lawn (read: gopher field) behind. Saskia had flown down from Boise, Elwood from the Flathead rez, and both had been joined by symbolic cousin Will and half sister Robin. There were others, too numerous to name.

Chelle had driven up with us from her temporary home—our house. She'd recovered most of her buoyancy, except for short periods when she faded into dark silence. When that happened she usually took Samuel the cat and disappeared into her room.

Al would go on trial next spring or summer or fall, depending on the overbooked court calendars in the various jurisdictions where he'd been charged.

The publicity surrounding Ollie's plight had called forth a sister in Wyoming who'd lost track of him, and he'd already moved in with her and her husband on their ranch near Cheyenne.

Me? Business is slow, so I'm taking time off to put my life in order. Time to think over the past and present. Time to evaluate what my future may be.

I need to consider those who are dear to me; they are so easy to lose. To forget old animosities...well, except a few. I ain't no Saint Sharon. Never have been, never will be.

I'm just me, for better or worse.

Before us, the sun dipped below the horizon, and we released Ma's ashes into the sea she had so loved. I waited, hoping...

And finally there it was—the green flash. A rare phenomenon, and this one even rarer because it was shooting straight up from the sun's vanishing point. I'd seen it do this only twice before.

This one's for you, Ma. Especially for you.

About the Author

Marcia Muller has written many novels and short stories. She has won six Anthony Awards and a Shamus Award, and is also the recipient of the Private Eye Writers of America Lifetime Achievement Award as well as the Mystery Writers of America Grand Master Award (their highest accolade). She lives in northern California with her husband, mystery writer Bill Pronzini. You can visit her on Facebook at FB.com/MarciaMullerAuthor.

MONDAY, DECEMBER 18

2:47 a.m.

An old man stands at one of the display windows of a jewelry store in San Francisco's exclusive Marina district. He is tall and muscular, his face nut brown and deeply furrowed, and his long gray hair is tied back in a ponytail under his knit cap, falling over the collar of his flannel shirt. His jeans are faded but clean; his athletic shoes are scuffed, well used.

It is late, but he is not tired; with every advancing year he requires less and less sleep, as if his body is greedy to soak up every bit of life remaining to it. If even a few moments of that time should measure up to his earlier years, he will be rich in the experiences he treasures.

He has traveled here to San Francisco from his home on the Flathead Indian Reservation in Montana to visit his daughter and her husband for the Christmas holiday. San Francisco is not a city he has visited often, although the few times he did, he was impressed with it. For a number of years—long ago—he lived in New York City, which was necessary for his work. Then a young man, he had delighted in its brashness and energy, but when he returned to the reserve in Montana its serenity had comforted him. Now he is intrigued by this city that seems to be so many different things to such a diverse population.

Tonight he has gone out for his customary walk and is contemplating a Christmas gift for his daughter. Those aquamarine earrings would please her, complement her black hair and dark eyes. Color is of primary importance to him, an artist of some renown.

His daughter: also a gift—to him. The child he never knew he had until she sought him out a few years ago at his small home in St. Ignatius on the rez. "I need to trace my family's roots," she'd told him. "I need to know who I am."

At first he'd been gruff with her, sent her away with orders to assemble her thoughts. His standard response when actually he needed to assemble *his*. But then she'd returned, and when all the twists and turns of their complicated lives had been sorted out, they'd realized they were father and daughter. Of course, mere blood ties are not all that's required to forge a true relationship. But they'd worked at its creation, he and his newfound child, and now—along with her amazing extended family of relatives and friends—he is part of something larger and better than himself.

The earrings, yes, he decides. He'll return for them in the morning. He moves along the display window, looking for a gift for his son-in-law—a kind, gentle man, but what the tribes used to call a warrior when circumstances warrant it. Come to think of it, his daughter is a warrior too.

A watch—yes! His son-in-law's current one looks shabby and out-of-date. What if it fails him? Much of the man's professional life depends on split-second timing. A good, well-styled watch, but not one of those foolish ones that spit out useless data just because they are designed to. His son-in-law has at his disposal far more sophisticated and reliable devices than those.

Of course, the Christmas shopping is far from completed. There are two cats in the household, and cats always enjoy treats. There is a housekeeper—a handsome woman of a certain age—who divides her time between his daughter's home and that of her best friend. And others of the couple's friends who have welcomed him and made him feel a part of their circle. Not to mention those on the reservation who urged him to make this extended trip.

So much shopping. And wrapping. And mailing. But what else has he to do with the fortune he's amassed over the years?

So much pleasure in finally having a reason to do so.

Noises on the formerly silent, empty street interrupt his thoughts. Hard heels slapping on the pavement in a manner that reminds him of old Nazi war movies he's seen on TV. They are coming from the west, the direction in which his daughter's house lies. Coming close to him.

He turns away from the display window, peers into the gloom, but is immediately blinded by spots of glaring light. They bob and weave, making it impossible for him to fix on anything behind them. Flashlights, of course. But why flashlights...?

A low, almost imperceptible growl reaches his ears. A human growl.

His flesh ripples. He has heard such growls before, on the rez long ago when opposing factions allowed their passions to escalate to rage. Instinctively he whirls and tries to run, but a hand is upon his right shoulder, staying him. And now they are dragging him into an areaway between two stores, getting him off the street.

"Dirty Indian," a rough voice says close to his ear. "What're you doing in our neighborhood?"

"I am . . ." But he can't choke out the words.

"Gonna rob the jewelry store, probably." Another hand grabs his left arm, shakes it painfully.

"That's what you guys do when you come to our city, isn't it? Break into places, steal like the savages you are."

And then the blows begin to fall—on his head, shoulders, back. Hard shoes kick his legs, a fist slams into his abdomen and doubles him over. He slides down, smacking his forehead on the pavement.

The last things he hears are the words, "The only good Indian is a dead Indian." Tires are swishing on the pavement and the rough voice calls, "Come on, guys, let's get outta here!"

The last thing he sees is a gold watch protruding from a white shirt cuff above the hand that relinquishes him.

4:08 a.m.

Hy and I are used to receiving urgent phone calls in the middle of the night, most of them requiring immediate action. But a ring of the doorbell at this hour? That was both unusual and alarming. Few people have our physical address.

Hy was at the ready, reaching for the .45 he keeps in his nightstand. I put a cautioning hand on his shoulder and said, "It's probably Elwood. I heard him go out on one of his late-night rambles a few hours ago. He might've forgotten his key."

As I caught up my heavy terrycloth robe, my husband was already clad in his, gun held low at his side. "Let's hope that's all this is." As we started down the stairway, he added, "I love your dad, McCone, but why don't we just pin the key to his jacket?"

"He'd probably forget it was there. Nobody on Moose Lane in St. Ignatius locks his or her house."

I'd left the porch light of our Spanish-style house on, knowing Elwood would be out rambling, and I could see burly shapes through the glass panes beside the door. The back of my neck prickled. Those were cop shapes; something was very wrong. I disabled the security system and threw the door open. The local officer on the beat, Winifred Sighesio, and her occasional partner Jeff Stacey stood there, faces tense with discomfort, and in an uncharacteristic gesture, Sighesio put her hand on my arm.

"May we come in?" she asked.

"Of course." I motioned them toward the living room.

Elwood. It has to have something to do with Elwood.

We all remained standing while Sighesio said, "An old man was not far from here an hour and a half ago, badly beaten, unconscious, with a possible concussion and multiple broken bones. Shabbily dressed, looked to be Native American. One of the EMTs found your card"—she nodded to me—"in his pocket. Your home, office, and cell numbers and this address were written on the back."

"Elwood!" His name slipped out between the fingers I'd pressed to my lips. Hy had slipped the .45 into the pocket of his robe; he put both arms around me and pulled me back against his chest.

"A pro bono client, maybe?" Stacey said. "I was there at the time, bringing in a psycho case, and I got a glance at the guy—a derelict. I don't know what you're doing passing out one of your cards to a filthy homeless guy, but—"

"He's my father, goddamn it!" I blinked back tears. Through them I could see the cop's eyes sizing up our large living room with its buttery leather furnishings, fireplace, and big flat-screen TV. How, his expression asked, could a raggedy old Indian fit into such a place?

"Where is my father?" I asked.

"SF General's trauma unit," Sighesio said.

"How is he? What are his injuries?"

"From what the EMTs could tell me, he has a broken arm, femur, ribs, and a possible concussion. He lost a lot of blood and hasn't regained consciousness."

Hy asked Sighesio more closely about how Elwood had been found. A passing motorist on his early commute to Silicon Valley spotted him in an areaway next to a jewelry store and called 911 on his mobile phone. She glanced down at the card she held. "Dennis Yee. He lives not far from you, is a software designer for Alfa, Inc."

One of the larger companies in the Valley.

I asked, "Was my father robbed?"

"Apparently not. His wallet contained quite a bit of cash."

"And did it look like any credit cards were missing?"

"There was only one—American Express, showing it was issued in 2002."

That was typical Elwood—one credit card, and I'd bet he paid it off in full every month.

"Any other evidence on the scene?"

"Blood smears indicating he was dragged from where he was attacked farther into the areaway."

"Bloody footprints?"

"No."

"What about witnesses?" I asked.

"As you know, that block of Chestnut Street is pretty densely populated with businesses, restaurants, and residential quarters above them. We're going to canvass it, but"—she threw out her arms helplessly—"we're so shorthanded."

"D'you know who the sergeant assigned to the case is?"

"Not yet."

"Well, maybe he or she may be willing to accept help on the task?"

"I would say you have an excellent chance of having your offer accepted."

"Now just wait a minute!" Stacey blurted. "Department regulations specifically forbid—"

Sighesio put her hand to her forehead. "Go away, Jeff."

She mutely pointed outside to where their black-and-white was parked.

"But—"

"Just *go*!"

He went, but not without shooting her an evil look.

"He needs sensitivity training," she apologized. "He's young, but if he doesn't grow up fast, his sorry ass ain't gonna be with the PD much longer. You folks want a ride to SFG?"

"No, we'll drive," I said.

"Well, be careful."

5:37 a.m.

I was no stranger to the SF General campus, but the new Zuckerberg Trauma Center dwarfed the older buildings at the foot of Potrero Hill. The public had approved an eight-hundred-and-some-thousand bond measure a few years ago, but that amount had only covered construction costs. Then Mark Zuckerberg, creator of Facebook, and his wife, Dr. Priscilla Chan, stepped in, donating seventy-five million to equip and furnish the facility.

Fewer years ago than I care to remember, I'd been a patient at the old trauma center, first in a coma and then in a locked-in state in which I was fully aware but unable to speak, move, or communicate in any way. Fortunately for me, the hospital's excellent staff—and later the staff at the rehab center the hospital referred me to—brought me back to the woman I'd once been, and I feel an intense loyalty to both the hospital and the center. Hy and I have directed a number of our philanthropic efforts their way—but nothing like those of Zuckerberg and Chan, whom we greatly admire.

Hy let me off at the door of the trauma center and went off to find a place to park. I joined the line for emergency room visitors, but one of the admitting personnel motioned me over; he was a man who'd befriended and visited me frequently when I was in my locked-in state.

The man took charge and cut through the standard waiting time of nearly an hour, and soon Hy and I were speaking with Dr. David Stiles, the neurosurgeon assigned to Elwood's case. As Sighesio had indicated, Elwood's condition was bad. He was in the intensive care unit and was not allowed visitors.

"He's strong for a man his age," Stiles said. "Do you have any idea of when he was born, Ms. McCone?"

"I don't know exactly, but I can get the information on the...from other relatives tomorrow." I'd almost said "on the moccasin telegraph," which would require too much explanation to this straightforward man of science.

"Your father's bone density appears to be good, but we're going to run tests to be sure. The breaks in the femur, the left arm, and the clavicle have been set. The ribs"—he shrugged—"all we could do was tape them."

He paused.

Oh God, here it comes!

"The most serious problem is that your father is suffering from traumatic brain injury. Do you know what that is?"

"I ought to. I was a patient here when I had locked-in syndrome."

"Ah—I thought your name was familiar. You're something of a legend around here." He went on, "Here's what we're doing: CT scans, which will reveal if he has suffered a subdural hematoma; other standard tests. If a blood clot has formed, surgery may be necessary."

"What about permanent brain damage?"

"At this point we can't hazard a guess, particularly at the onset. The brain is tricky, and it varies its tricks from day to day. Your father may have suffered major brain damage, or he could wake up one morning and ask for a cup of coffee. Let's hope he is built of the same strong stuff you are."

We talked some more about Elwood's injuries, and, since we couldn't see him yet, against my wishes Hy and I left for home. "I wanted to stay," I told him.

"There's nothing for you to do at the hospital, but plenty at home."

I realized that it was now morning across the entire continent, and I had to face the unpleasant task of notifying my family members.

7:01 a.m.

Saskia Blackhawk, my birth mother, had become close to Elwood in recent years, so initially I phoned her in Boise. She expressed shock, then indignation, and flew into her full lawyer mode. "I'll be at SFO on the first available flight and come directly to the hospital," she told me.

Saskia is an attorney for Indian rights who has argued before the US Supreme Court and won every case. If Elwood's attackers were ever found, her rage and legal expertise would make them pay the maximum penalty.

"Before I let you go," she added, "please don't call your mother. It's best I break the news myself."

"Why? Is Ma—"

"Just don't tell her. I'll explain when I see you."

Next I called the reigning gossip queen of the moccasin telegraph in St. Ignatius, Jane Nomee, and asked her to spread the word about the attack but to caution everyone that my father wasn't up to having visitors just yet and that no one should report the attack to the press or police. The moccasin telegraph is a loosely linked group of our people who are devoted to circulating information about all things Indian throughout the nation. Once, they claim, it operated on smoke signals—and maybe it did—but these days the Internet and smartphones transmit the necessary information. Jane, who is a devotee of TV crime shows, agreed to get moving on Elwood's mishap, and soon, I was sure, the wires would be humming.

My most difficult call was to Will Camphouse in Tucson. He wasn't a relative of mine in the white-world sense, but—as he often claimed—maybe he was in the cosmic sense. Whatever, he was the closest thing to a brother I had in the Indian part of my family.

Will said, "I already know. Robin called me."

Robin Blackhawk, my half sister in Berkeley. Of course she knew; Saskia had probably phoned her to ask for a ride from SFO to SFG.

Will added, "You want me to come up there?"

"Not necessary—not yet."

"Well, don't hesitate to ask; I've just wrapped up a big campaign and have some time off coming." He was creative director at a large Tucson ad agency.

I closed my eyes, picturing hordes of the descendants of Chief Tendoy—leader of the Lemhi Shoshone from 1863 until his death in 1907—convening at the hospital and in the Marina district, lobbying for

Indian rights. The Shoshone are normally a gentle people, skilled in coping with adversity and hostility, but they've been pushed around enough by white society and the US government to go into explosive mode when circumstances warrant it.

I said, "I think it's a good idea to keep as many of our people away from here as we can till we know more."

Will understood. "You know what, I think I'll use the time to go up to Montana and try to keep the tribe under control."

The rest of my calls were not so difficult: My adoptive brother John, who lives in a downtown high-rise here in the city, is fond of Elwood and my Indian family, and said he'd be on call for anything they needed. My nephew Mick Savage, chief researcher at the agency, had seen the attack reported on the morning news and had put out a staff bulletin, and was already working the case. My go-to couples, Hank Zahn and Anne-Marie Altman, and Rae Kelleher and Ricky Savage, had heard about it too. Then calls began pouring in from friends they'd contacted. I'd had no idea how many people cared about me and mine.

9:08 a.m.

After a while e-mails and calls from the media began flooding in, and a few of the more audacious members of the press came creeping around our house. So much for our imagined anonymity. Hy immediately posted M&R guards on the property. I spoke to Mick about our building downtown on New Montgomery, and he said he'd ordered the security staff to clamp it down tight, but already a freelance journalist with a video cam had somehow gotten in and frightened one of the office cleaning staff when she found him hiding in one of the utility closets.

Shortly after I finished speaking with Mick, a Sergeant Priscilla Anders from the SFPD assault division called and asked if she could come over and interview us about Elwood. I agreed, did a quick spiff-up, and greeted her at the door. Anders was an attractive woman of about sixty, wearing a conservative gray pantsuit to match her conservatively cut gray hair; a delicate silver necklace and matching bracelet were her only adornments. She showed me her identification and then followed me to the living room, where she accepted coffee from the pot Hy had just brewed and got right down to business.

"Your father normally resides where?" she asked me, snapping open a spiral-bound notebook.

"In St. Ignatius, Montana, on the Flathead Reservation."

"He is here visiting for the holidays?"

"Yes. He arrived two days ago and intends to stay through the New Year."

"Mr. Farmer is in his eighties?"

"That's correct. I should shortly have his exact age and date of birth from one of the other relatives."

"I'd appreciate it if you would let me know. What does Mr. Farmer do in Montana? Is he retired?"

"No. He's a nationally known painter and also tutors in various schools in the area near the reservation."

Anders looked at her notes. I had the feeling she

already knew most of the information I'd provided, but was checking for accuracy's sake.

"Do you know if your father has any enemies?"

"In San Francisco? He's only been here two days."

"Someone who may have followed him from Montana?"

"That's extremely doubtful. He's a beloved figure throughout the state."

"Could the attack have been directed at you or Mr. Ripinsky?" She nodded at Hy, who was sitting quietly in a chair near the fireplace. "Perhaps someone intent on doing harm to your father as a way of harming you?"

"...I hadn't thought of that."

"Given the nature of your business, you must have made a number of enemies."

"Well, yes. But I doubt our relationship to Elwood is widely known."

"Are you sure of that?"

"My father is a very private man. And my husband and I are private, too. In our personal lives."

"Yet you seem to have garnered more than your fair share of publicity, both local and national."

Hy moved restively—a caution not to give in to the emotional storm that he knew was building within me. To Anders he said, "My wife and I don't seek out attention, Sergeant. Our aim, as simple as it may seem to others, is to create better circumstances for our clients."

"And I suppose these clients are always on the right side of the law?"

"One or two who aren't may slip through our background checks. But the checks are very thorough, and in the unlikely event we find someone's misrepresented himself or herself to us, we have a clause in our contract that releases us from their employ and"—he smiled slyly—"allows us to keep any retainer they may have paid us. That's the point where the undesirables put down their pens and walk out."

I said, "Can we please get back to the assault on my father?"

"Of course." Anders nodded. "So if the attack wasn't aimed at harming the two of you, do you suppose it was simply random?"

"That's my take on it," I replied.

"A random attack in an affluent neighborhood upon an individual who didn't look as if he belonged there."

"An especially vicious attack," I said. "Possibly by someone motivated by racial hatred."

Anders smiled as if I were a school kid who had given the right answer to a tricky question. "That's the primary angle I'm planning to pursue the crime from." She stood, briskly snapping her notebook shut. "I'll keep you informed."

I shut the door behind her and said to Hy, "Cold woman, huh?"

"Yeah."

"Why, d'you think?"

"Could be many things."

"Not racial prejudice. I can sniff that out instantly. Not because she resents our financial status; her clothing and jewelry tell me she uses what she earns well or has inherited money."

"Could be that she doesn't like dealing with a firm like M&R. We've snatched the solutions to prized investigations out of the SFPD's hands a few times."

Alex the cat entered the room, his tail switching, and sniffed the place where the inspector had been sitting.

I said, "She hates cats?"

We both burst into tension-easing laughter, and then the landline rang. I picked up. A familiar voice, usually maternal but distinctively not so at the moment, said, "What the hell are you doing at home? Get your asses over here!"

"Ma?" The name came out weakly.

"Your father is lying here in the ICU, the rest of the family has arrived, and what are you doing?"

So much for no one telling her.

"We've been talking with the police."

"Are you done with them?"

"Yes, just now."

"Then get your asses *over here!*" She hung up.

I met Hy's eyes. His were vaguely amused.

"Okay," I said. "Okay, let's go."